Cynan Jones was born in Wales in 1975. His first novel, *The Long Dry*, was published in 2006 and went on to win a Betty Trask Award from the Society of Authors. The book has since been translated into Italian, Arabic and French.

Other short work has been variously published, and the author was selected as the Hay Festival nominee for the 2008 Scritture Giovani project.

This is his second novel.

Everything
I Found
on the Beach

Cynan Jones

PARTHIAN

Parthian
The Old Surgery
Napier Street
Cardigan
SA43 1ED
www.parthianbooks.co.uk

First published in 2011
© Cynan Jones
All Rights Reserved

ISBN 978-1-906998-49-3

The publisher acknowledges the financial support of the Welsh
Books Council.

Cover design: James Fleming © gigantic-design.com
Typeset by Lucy Llewellyn

Printed and bound by Dinefwr Press, Llandybïe

For Coram, Alex, Tom,
and Emlyn Llewelyn, my brother.

'He had said, "I am a man," and that meant certain things... It meant that he was half insane and half god.'

John Steinbeck, *The Pearl*

Prologue

He watched the coast receding,

the lights that were coming on in the late afternoon blinking and then dropping in the stretched distance.

The man was in a kind of numb, tired shock.

'What did I do?' he asked. There was just this widening grey sea out there and the rain, blurring the last visible lights now.

There was no choice. I had to do that. I didn't have a choice.

He considered what he had done.

I didn't have a choice, he told himself.

He stood on the deck for a long while and just watched the coast thinning and receding. But he couldn't get rid of the question.

'What is it that I've done?'

The sergeant was on the beach

and looked down at the body and the younger policeman Morgan was with him and it was the first time for him, seeing something so severe.

The body had most of the fingers of one hand off and there was a big wound to the face and out through the back of the head.

The tide had lapped up on the body and the salt water had swelled the edges of the big wound. It was early, but the birds had been awake and the eyes were already gone. It was really severe to look at.

The owlish man got out of the taxi that he'd just rolled up along the little slip to the beach and came down the slip and called out to the young policeman.

The sergeant looked up tiredly. 'Christ,' said the sergeant. 'Keep him away.'

The young policeman saw a small crab scuttle from under the face of the body and it seemed to dislodge the balance of the head so it rolled slightly, as if it moved in its sleep. It made the young policeman feel sick.

'What have you got, Morgan?'

The young policeman went up to the owlish man who was standing by the blue and white tape the other police had put up. The owlish man was pecky and curious looking.

'What have you got?' he asked again.

Morgan shrugged. 'We don't know yet. We're not sure.' He looked very pale and sick.

The sand beach was long and slightly curved and the water hissed where the edge of the tide petered out. They were putting up a screen now around the body and the owlish man was looking, trying to see whatever he could.

'When did you find him?' asked the owlish man.

'Right early. Someone walking a dog.'

The old guy had been walking his dog and described how the dog had run up to the corpse and scattered the birds and the idea of the birds pecking at the face made Morgan sick inside again.

'You look paler than when I picked you up the other night,' said the owlish taxi driver, trying to be light.

The owlish man could just see the legs of the body now. The legs looked distraught and wet like the tide had been over them and he noticed the kind of shapeless deadness to them as if they weren't real.

'Any explanation? Nothing on him?' asked the man.

'No.' The policeman had swallowed down his sickness once more. 'No. Unless the tide took it. He could have been washed up. We're not sure yet.'

'Didn't happen here then?'

'We don't know,' said the policeman. He thought about the fingers missing and about the big wound to

3

the face. He wanted to go back to the body. It was easier actually being by it and looking at it like a big fact. There was something unreal and factual and more dead about the body that way and it was easier to deal with.

The sergeant called up to the young policeman.

'I shouldn't be talking to you,' Morgan said to the owlish man. He got more formal. 'I can't give you any information at the present time. I'll have to ask you to leave the scene.'

Other men had parked up and were coming down the slipway in white forensics suits onto the beach. There was something weird about the beach that looked like it had been busier at one time, some time in the distant past. But then it had been abandoned, fallen out of favour.

'You don't know who it is then?' asked the owlish man.

The young policeman had turned to go back.

'No.' He had the thought of the gulls pulling at the dead face. 'We've got no idea who it is yet.'

Some hours down the coast the woman opened the envelope and in the moment when she saw inside it felt this terrible and overwhelming relief at the answer and finality there, and then the emotion hit her and flooded out every other thing.

Part One

The sun seemed to drop quickly

this time of year and it made an unattractive light against the gates of the slaughterhouse.

Grzegorz waited with a group of other men. He was just off shift and he still had rimes of dried blood around his fingernails and the smell of the place was still on him. He was seemingly wakened to the smell all over again by being outside, as if he smelt it for the first time. It was crisp, cold almost. He didn't feel that he had come anywhere. He was tired. It was cold. Just like Poland.

Grzegorz watched the light slide down the zinc gates and took the cigarette his friend offered him and they smoked like the others, waiting for the bus and watching the trucks go in to the factory. There were eight men, and every now and then, with the fickle breeze, they got the stench of the incinerator. It was getting cold quickly. It was that time of year still.

When the bus arrived the guy driving pulled up on the other side of the road and beeped twice and still smoking the men got on. The bus seemed too small for the eight men and the driver. The driver told them they might as well get comfortable. He said the trip would be at least an hour.

Grzegorz was still angry at the argument. Another one today. He couldn't tell what he had done but the line manager really had it in for him. He was tired of that. He thought he had left that behind in Poland.

'They just want to keep you constantly down,' he thought. 'Keep you scared. So you just get on and follow the line. Just like those stupid obedient cows who wander along the line into the stun, as if it was the only way their life would ever have gone. Well, I'm over that. You see a chance, you have to take it.'

Some of the men had set up a card game and they were passing round a bottle of something home-made. Grzegorz took a swig. The alcohol was vicious and orangey and amateur. Underneath the noise on the bus there was this odd sense among the men. Grzegorz thought back to Poland and being picked up for the village football team as a kid, this sense of imposed mirth existing over a nervousness before the game.

He looked down at his phone, flicked through the pictures of Ana and his two sons. He thought of the fee, what it could represent, here in this country let alone in Poland. This is for them, he thought. This could change it all for them. He looked for a long while at the picture of his wife.

'What did you tell her?' asked his friend, nodding down at the phone. Grzegorz realised he'd been on some kind of small absence when the noise and motion of the bus had seemed to fade.

'I told her I was working a triple shift,' Grzegorz said. He hid the picture on his phone.

His friend nodded. 'Me too,' he said. He dug in his bag. 'Look at the quantity of sandwiches she made me.'

The men laughed and sat eating the sandwiches and smoking and drinking and through the windows of the moving bus the last bit of light seemed to have an unnatural persistence.

The men laughed and drank but as they went along Grzegorz thought of the long space of the beach, the flat sands and that sense of peace when he was cockle digging. He could never afford land, but the beach had a common right and he could work it. It would be the closest thing to a farm. He just needed to set himself up.

It was over an hour before they got to the dock and the men got gratefully off the bus. The mood was different now.

A guy came out of the shed and talked to them in Polish and then the whole group of them went into the shed.

Grzegorz remembered what his friend had said.

9

The only tricky bit is the boat, but it's simple. It's like steering a plough really. It's the only difficult part.

Grzegorz stood there with the others listening to a man who spoke to them from behind a desk that looked odd in the otherwise empty boatshed. Grzegorz's English was still poor and he understood only some of what was said, but then the Pole who had spoken to them outside barked out the translation. He was skin-headed and brutal looking. A football hooligan. Grzegorz felt a sense of unrealness, this new and hollow fear at the idea of the black sea they had seen from the bus. They'd been asked once and simply outside the shed if they wanted to back out. 'Once you're in the shed you're in everything,' said the Pole. 'You back out then, there'll be consequences.' No one had backed out.

The men went up individually and showed their identification to the man behind the desk and he took the passports and ID cards in this strange formal way and put them all together in a strong box. 'You'll get them when you get back,' he said.

For each of them that went up, the man behind the desk flashed a square of paper. This visible change came over the man that had gone up then and they moved off.

The skinhead stood close to the desk, just out of the light. He was like some kind of unnerving scavenger. Grzegorz felt him almost, rather than saw him, had this rip of gall go through him at the irreversibility of this thing he was doing. For a moment he had the taste of the horrible liquor come up in his mouth again, but he swallowed it down. It was like the sick feeling he had as a child before he used to jump off the bridge into the cold pool of the river by his grandparents' farm. He was one of the youngest of the kids who played, and always the first to be made to jump. He swallowed the fear back, the same way he used to, with this childish determination to do something he knew was dangerous and stupid. For what? For the chance to be something.

Grzegorz stepped up and handed over his passport to the man and looked up at the skin-headed man trying not to show the nervous rush that was going through him.

The man looked at the outline of the eagle on the passport then at the name, then ran his finger down a list in front of him with this surreal-seeming officiousness. Then he drew out a photograph and showed Grzegorz a picture of his wife pushing the pram. This sick feeling came up hard in Grzegorz.

The skin-headed Pole was acting as translator.

'Can you drive a boat?'

Grzegorz nodded numbly.

'Yes. I can drive a boat.'

Hold sat on the upturned crate and cut down the spine of the fish and let the boat bob and tremble around him in the water. He held the fish down on the board and cut behind the gills and then turned the knife stiffly in the flesh and cut through the rib bones and drew off the fillet. Intact but for this loin of it gone, the fish looked still alive it was so fresh.

Hold sliced away the spurs of rib that had come off in the smooth cut of the fillet and threw them into the water; then he pared the flesh finally from the skin and threw the skin too into the water. Then he cut the fillet and took up the pieces one by one and ate them richly, chewing and savouring them.

It was the early mixed up warmth of spring, and the colder breeze could not get into the boat the way it faced, so the space inside was warm and was one of the first warmths of the year to him.

He ate the fish and got up and took the boiled kettle from the gimballed stove and made a black coffee and sat back on the crate in the strange created warmth and felt the boat and felt the sea get up slightly beneath him.

Holden looked at the knife and cleaned it on his trouser sleeve and tested its edge with his thumbprint and tried it against the hairs of his arm and looked up from the boat at the cliffs and at the pale kittiwakes circling off them.

Three years ago, Danny had died and had left him this knife. Hold had taken the knife but there was inside him the sense that he was keeping it in trust for Jake, and that he would pass it on when the boy was old enough.

It was as if the continued use of the knife was vital in keeping the sense of his friend around him. He'd give it to Jake. He'd made that decision straight off. He'd give it to Danny's boy Jake when he got old enough.

When Grzegorz brought his child

back newly from the hospital there was a celebration. Already, the traditional red ribbon he had been given when they went off to the hospital in the taxi was tied around the little boy's wrist. Everyone held his new son, and it was like delivering him to some huge, surrogate family.

He'd waited at the door for a moment, as if getting his breath, letting his wife go in with the baby to the initial greetings. 'This is not right,' Grzegorz thought, 'it is not right to bring a son into this. He should have a real home, a place better than this.' He stood in the doorway of the bleak place and looked blankly at the artless graffiti that went across the broken brick wall in front of him. Polish out.

He thought of the boy taking his first steps here, uttering his first words. 'No,' Grzegorz thought. 'It is okay now, he is too small for anything. But I have to get out before he starts to grow up, before he walks. I want his first steps to be around a table that is ours. That belongs to us. I want him to have a room of his own with his brother. I didn't come here for this.' He felt a strange, tired relief and joy and emptiness.

He went upstairs. His son was in the big maternal arms of one of the heavier older women and he saw his wife tired, uncertain, this look of things slipping away. That should be my grandmother, holding him there, my new son. He looked at his wife and met her eyes. He looked fascinated at his wife's strangely deflated stomach after all the months of fullness. She was like a child against the big heavy woman. 'This should be happier,' he thought. 'This should be happier than this.' He thought of the humiliating, horrible thing of the waters breaking there in the room full of people.

A man came in and put three ducks down on the table. Grzegorz looked at the birds, limp and distraught, river mud in amongst the oiled colours of their feathers. He looked at the very orange legs of the wild ducks and wondered, detachedly, how the man could have caught them. And then the man put down bottles on the table and there came a sudden activity, glasses banging on the table, the birds swept up.

At the beginning there had been exactly this kind

of vibrant energy to the house. There was the sense of the beginning of a party, of some great feast a big family had come together for. There was a common purpose to all the people that had arrived, that had come on the two buses, the men to jobs allocated them by the agency. Then the weight of it had sunk in.

He did not know they would be there for so long, stuck, suspended somehow in this no-man's-land between Poland and what they had held as an ideal new world. It was more than a year now. The baby, product of that first new vibrant energy, a momentous piece of life that they felt was a sign of the newness and change of everything, came now not with celebration but as an extra weight. He had bought into a vision of this country that did not fit. He was unnerved by the dullness of the buildings, the latent fatigue of the place, colourless shops with broken signage. It didn't tally with the view he'd had of the place. He was perturbed by some strange lack he could not pin down here.

He felt at the same time this tired, trapped fear alongside this great and in some way desperate gratitude for this accidental family around him. 'They are good people; we're all in the same boat here,' he thought. 'All reliant on the agency still, as if they held us in some grip.' Because of the break when they'd laid them off for three weeks, he hadn't quite clocked up the twelve months' unbroken work that would make him eligible for benefits, so he couldn't move out of the house yet, not on the money he had. There was talk that the agency had organised this break deliberately so they didn't have a choice but to accept the work and the stoppages in their pay cheques – the deductions for rent, for the transport to work that was laid on, for house cleaning, though none of them had ever seen a cleaner. But it's just talk, thought Grzegorz. We're responsible for ourselves.

He was handed a glass and took a big, long drink. 'We have to keep moving forward,' thought Grzegorz. 'We think we have no choice. But this is the land of choice. We can't just blame the situation all the time. We have to take the next step.' He looked for his wife. She had gone from the room. The baby was still with the old woman.

In the first mild blur of alcohol the hard edges of his worry smoothed off. 'Did I make all the wrong choices?' he thought. 'We couldn't have stayed though. We could never have stayed.' He held his new son and drank, his older boy withdrawn and strangely displaced, confused by the placatory attention people were showing him, pointing at the new baby. They were talking to him. 'You have to say "brother" here. You can't call him your brat like in Poland. It means something else here.' They laughed. 'Learn to call him your "brother". You're not in Poland now!' He didn't understand; besides, the activity in the kitchen

16

startled the boy. He was always withdrawn, self-contained. Grzegorz watched him and thought back to the boy's first birthday.

They'd put him down on the carpeted floor and round him set out the traditional things. A book, a banknote, his wife's sister's rosary and a vodka glass, the *kieliszek*, all spread out equally from the child. Then they waited, tongue in cheek but with that strange whisper of conviction superstitions can have, to see what he reached for first. Whether he would be, in his future, an intellectual, a businessman, a priest or a drunk. Of course, it's possible to be all of them at once, his friend had said. That had made them laugh. You just need four hands! His son had reached for the book. 'That's not a good sign,' thought Grzegorz. He felt inadequate. Grzegorz felt it immediately as something he would not be able to help with.

The women were rolling out the dough for the *pierogi*, the small stuffed dumplings, cutting out circles with a glass and dropping in the fillings then folding them and pinching them closed. Some of the other children were helping and there was a long row of parcels starting to line up.

The women took the ducks and drained the blood off into cups and the air stank as they burned the last fine feathers off the duck on the gas ring and the kitchen filled with an acrid tang. Still the boy stared. Grzegorz watched the skins tauten in the flame and

17

the buds of down char and desiccate and the women's fat soft hands brush them off. He looked down at his new little son, at the delicate red ribbon, then at his older boy who stood watching while the other children ran round catching the plucked feathers that inevitably escaped and floated round in the crowded light of the kitchen.

The boy stared. Grzegorz thought his son must have some faint memory of the big farm table, the low ceiling. Of the warm milky smell of the soft old woman that was being blurred in his mind amongst the matrons of this house, was turning into nothing more than a suspicion that he once knew someone special. Poland would be a strange thing to him, a distant awareness that would perhaps fade and become nothing more than an historical fact as he grew. With all the Polish around him, nothing had really changed. But there was no place of focus for the boy now, and, looking at him, Grzegorz felt the boy would always carry this sense of having been removed from something and that he would never understand it.

He nodded as one of the women lifted the boy and stood him on a chair where he held on to the unit alongside her, staring at the process of the ducks, surrounded by the noise and festivity. The boy watched the women pour the white vinegar into the blood to stop it clotting, twitched his nose with the sharp smell of it and poked his finger curiously into the blood. Then he watched as one of the men took the big abattoir knife from his holdall and cut up the ducks, now these strange naked, riddled creatures, and quartered them onto the board.

Grzegorz took up his new son and went out. The house was always crowded and small but it seemed to close in on him. He seemed to be carrying too many confusing emotions, and just didn't know how to feel. It was like he couldn't settle on one feeling. This was all new. He thought of the wide eyes of the boy watching the ducks being quartered. There was no resting place of family, of places he knew. There had been for the first boy, and he had taken him from them. Now, he had to get it right for them both.

Grzegorz was still partly stunned. He had thought the hospitals here would be so much better than at home, but he was horrified. The machines here were newer, the buildings better kept. But he'd suffered this unshakeable feeling that they were being herded like cattle, going through this numerical process. There didn't seem to be any doctors about, any nurses. Not like when his first son was born. At least there had been people to help, always. And he knew the score. They'd saved what złotys they could and when they went into the hospital paid off the right people, so the care and concern they got was good and consistent. You got what you paid for. But here there had been an impersonal thing he couldn't get used to. He was horrified by the farm-like ward, had tried to pay a nurse to get his wife a room, anywhere, just some place they could be away from people for a while, for the first few hours of his new baby's life, before going back into the house. The nurse had just looked at him bewildered, and he didn't have the English to explain.

He lay down in the women's room with his wife. She was tired, brittle looking. From the women's room, they smelled the stock making in the kitchen below, heard the simmering of the building celebration. People stayed away to give them time. They were thankful for that. There were people in the hospital, there were people here. They just wanted space together to take in this massive new thing.

Grzegorz looked down at the exquisite new thing of his son and felt this strange and terrible pride. The boy threw out his arms and cried. From somewhere, Grzegorz had the illusion of Christmas as the cloves and the allspice lifted through the room and the smell of the stock grew. He saw the ducks clearly in his grandfather's hand, the long low marsh. Remembered exactly the precious tin his grandmother kept the spices in. The boy cried feebly and his wife put him to her breast. 'The things we need are very simple,' thought Grzegorz. 'I want to have the things we need for them.'

Hold worked inshore the strings of prawn pots, bringing up the creels with the pot haul and letting the boat idle, anchored some by the weight of the string in the water. He was a few hundred metres off the shore and the sun had come round enough to light up the beach and it looked beautiful, and he thought there was something more determined in the way the coast looked in the colder months.

Much of the prawn fishing was done in these colder months and he emptied the prawns into the drum and they flicked and clicked and there was no rhyme or reason to why some of the pots had prawns and some none. He knew this very well, that there were no averages, no laws with fishing. He could imagine the prawns nibbling, testing, weighing the pot. Something had to make them want to go in, they had to be encouraged; but once they were in that was that. They were stuck with the decision.

Hold rebaited the pots that needed it with the scad and herring they had salted down and then he set the boat and played the string back out into the water and there was the comfortable rhythm of the engine and the splash of the creels rhythmically hitting the water.

He went cursorily through the drum and picked out the smallest prawns and threw them over the side, and wondered how they felt for that moment in the totally foreign element of the air; then he lifted some buckets of seawater and filled the drum and banged on the lid. He didn't believe in the unnecessary suffering of things and saw no purpose to letting the prawns suffocate blithely in the air. That was a very strong thing in Hold: his belief that a thing should not die nor be hurt without purpose. For this reason he didn't take the lobsters that were only just of size, knowing how slowly they grew, nor did he shoot things that were scarce, the hares and doves which he seemed to remember seeing all the time as a child but rarely saw now. Though he fished and shot, this was for a purpose and that he was engineer of the hurt inevitable he felt with great responsibility and that was a great driving force in him. It gave him a respect for life and for the right of things to exist. He felt we had come too far from this.

He played the strings out and then went on to the lobster pots that he had put out for the first time this season. In the first pot there was a big lobster and there was no reason for it on the fresh bait, and in the other pots, their spines stuck with weed and debris, were spider crabs, strangely early and again, for this, without reason to be there. He unloaded the lobster from the pot and put it in a tub, and then took out the spider crabs, their conkery shells crusted with acorn barnacles. He wondered whether the spider crabs being early was from some disturbance, perhaps flushed by the scallop dredgers out at sea, or some sign of unusual warming water. 'Ah,' thought Hold. 'There just aren't any rules. Just the rule that the sea will keep surprising you.'

In the kitchen, the boy helped the women throw the spices into the pot and then watched them take the deformed pieces of duck out from the water and shred off the meat, putting the offal to one side on a plate. The boy stared at it with a kind of enamoured disgust. 'For your Mama,' they said. 'It will help keep her strong after the baby.'

The boy helped throw the dried fruit into the soup, then they poured in the cups of rich black blood and then gradually the flour, and the boy watched as the soup slowly thickened.

Still there was an illusion of Christmas with the smells that had reached the sleeping room. Grzegorz looked down at the little red ribbon on the child's wrist. It was unnerving him. He thought it made the baby look as if it wore a price tag, as if somehow he was for sale. Part of him wanted to rip it away, to tear away the idea that there could be anything like an evil eye out there to be protected from. But he didn't feel he could defy superstition for one moment. It had been built into him too long ago. 'It's not being watched. It's being kept down,' he thought. 'I'll have to try and make a little more now. We can save more. We can get out of here to a place of our own.'

When the couple came back to the kitchen and saw the boy on the chair helping the women with the soup, Grzegorz almost choked with this cloth of thanks that seemed to cough up out of him from somewhere. He was filled with this great sense that they would make it, that they would get through all of this and be happy soon. That this was just a stop on the way. He reached for his wife's hand and held it, and for a moment just in this small gesture there was all this renewed hope.

One of the older women handed a plate to his wife and there was something almost religious about the act, as if of some great donation. She looked down at the duck offal.

'It'll keep you strong,' said the woman. Grzegorz saw the great pride in the woman's face.

The wave of hope broke and smashed over the stones of the facts. 'I'm still in Poland,' thought Grzegorz. Again, the boat of his emotions tipped in the waves. 'We can't move on while there is all of this, we can't become anything new.' He looked at all the Polish products around the place, sitting in the cooking smells, the familiarity of the sounds. He looked desperately out of the window at the wall opposite with the big graffiti, Polish out, but he didn't register it any more. He wanted to feel better at this incredible time.

'This is where we are now,' he thought. 'And we have to move on. Here. Poland has nothing for us.' He wanted so much to change things and to bring all these new things to his life. He was very desperate for that. 'I just need a chance,' he thought. He watched his wife eat up the small offal with her fingers, holding their tiny new son. Someone needs to give me a chance.

As he headed back in, Hold took five or

six of the fish and laid them on the gunwale. They were medium-sized fish and he held them down on the gunwale and descaled them with the back of the knife, working in little jerking strokes. Then he moved the descaled fish to a board on the gunwale and took off the flesh, working from the head down along the spine then slipping out the rib bones from the severed flanks and putting the fillets into a box. It was a rhythmic and calm process and he moved easily with the boat as it headed in and he could feel the course of the boat just with his body. He had taken bass and codling in the net and it was the bass he filleted.

When he had taken the fillets, he cut out the intestines into a pile. Then he cut off the translucent meat and the flaps of foily skin and cut the heads from the thick spines and threw all of that into one of the bait tubs for the pots. The bass had big heads for their size and this was good bait and lasted a long time in the pots in the water. He did this with a kind of mechanism and it was part of him to invent little rituals and to give himself small lectures.

Above him, a string of gulls had come on, and he flicked off the rich pile of intestines from the gunwale and the gulls dropped into the water after the sinking guts. In amongst the bright white adults, some of the gulls still had the juvenile plumage they would have until some summers further on. Hold had noticed how the younger gulls had rich brown eyes, with something almost mammalian in them, but that the older gulls' eyes were cold, yellow, as if something had gone out of them. Some of the adult gulls were so close he could see clearly the red spot on their beak that the chicks would tap to make them regurgitate food, and while he did not care for the yellow eyes, he liked this mechanism in them.

He hauled a bucket of water and washed the scales and the rust-like blood down off the gunwale and cleaned the cutting board and his knife then washed the blood and scales off his hands with the seawater, which was the best way. He could feel a chop starting in the sea that would mean the weather getting up in the next few days, the sea here filling with the beginnings of an energy nascent hundreds of miles away. Some Bahamian storm or seeming emotional reaction to change in pressure days away from here.

He could feel that there was great power and swell in the sea, though it was calm out on the water, and the lifting of the waves at the shore had the power of a prowling animal about it, and some male thing, like someone who hopes someone will fight them.

He took a long drink of clean water and cut a sliver off one of the fillets and chewed the virile and strong raw flesh and counted in his head, as he chewed, the likely take from the day's catch.

He got a percentage of the price of the fish at sale and a flat rate every time he took the boat out. The owner covered all the costs and handled the licence and never came out on the boat.

After getting fired from the fish factory, Hold had looked into trying to set up on his own boat but the sums were simply too big. It was getting started, that was the thing. If you didn't have anything you just couldn't start up.

He'd made the right choice with the factory. It would have been worse if Danny had gone. He was always a joker. That kind of thing came with his basic sense of adventure and it wasn't the first time Hold had taken the fall for him. But Danny had the wife and family. There was a lot of seasonal stuff about, but work wasn't easy round here. It was better that Hold took it on.

He gave up the bedsit and went into the caravan. That suited, with the work they were trying to get done on the house. Cara was furious with Danny for letting Hold take the fall, but what could you do? You couldn't get that furious with Danny, you never could.

He thought of it and smiled even now. There was an energy and hurry always as they loaded the trays of crabs onto the racks for the blast freezer, a compulsive clonking sound to the cooked pasty-like shells knocking together as they handled the crabs, a fresh baity smell. It was crazy work and it could easily breed a silliness and it was just one of those moments Danny was prone to.

When the guy came out of the blast freezer he was frosted, like he'd been dipped in wet sugar. He could hardly move. Funny as it was it could have killed him. His apron had been blasted out and stood solid, straight out like a shelf in front of him. That set the men off.

When the supervisor arrived it was pretty inevitable. The guys were still laughing, some of them uncontrollably. It was the apron. They just couldn't get over that.

'Who was it?'

'It was me,' Hold had said. That was that. But he laughed about it even now. That was Danny, he thought. I couldn't have let him lose his job.

After that he worked for two years in the cheese factory in the valley, and took the shift work that came with it and the pay which was good for the area. But it was futile, monotonous work that seemed to be nothing but moving cheese around. Not many people lasted long at it. Work's work, he had told himself, trying to get through it, setting up little purposes, timescales, the tricks we play on ourselves to get through things. But Danny dying had been a wake-up call, and he just couldn't do it any more. He couldn't pretend that he was going to work there in that way for years and save money then buy a boat that he could take out and make a little money on, fishing or taking out trips. Anything could take you. He knew that now. And he wouldn't do things he could see no value in or not get something back from, He looked at the knife which his friend had given him and he looked at it still in his hand and smiled at the thought of the apron again. The money he had was not very much. That was that. But he could cope with the things he did to get it.

He could hear the cattle lowing through the walls, this strange muted sound from the sheds where the vets rhythmically checked the animals, seemingly calm and oblivious. From home, Grzegorz knew how the smell would be in there. How the warm, manurey smell of cattle would be different to the sharp, chemical tang around him. There was something low and maternal about the sound to Grzegorz as he stood in the blood-letting bay, something that would not fit against the men in white overalls, the white rubber boots and white helmets, the strange medicalness of that. He was used to the idea of animals as products, but he was trying to adjust to the clinicality of it. Cows were better than sheep though. When the sheep came through there was something more startled to them, a horror in the number. It was more of a cull and the sheep seemed always to sense that with this contagious and wide fear. He'd heard someone say they killed twenty-five thousand sheep a week here. That didn't seem possible.

When the bigger animals came through the pen the sound was more that of a long queue. It reminded Grzegorz of waiting on the gangplank of the ferry when they came over, finally off the cramped bus after hours of travel. There was the odd sound of metal clanking, as now and then the cattle brushed the railings of the four-metre walkway. They didn't have the panicked, startled look of the lambs. They were droll. There was a checkpoint, and as the cows came through one of the men stopped each animal and checked its ear to see that the tag and passport corresponded and then moved it along up the ramp.

They came up droll and oblivious, with the kind of calm factuality of big, heavy animals, and one by one they stepped into the kill pen.

There was the grating sound of the metal end door as it slid up and the cow went in, then it clanged down and the animal, unable to move in the small pen, stayed calm. The first metal plate rose up onto the animal's nose and it seemed to sit down and crumple, as if it had chosen to rest for a while. Then the second plate came up onto the animal's chest and the cow shook for a few seconds then went still.

It was the strange, detached process of the electricity that Grzegorz could not get used to, the passivity of the whole thing. Then the side door of the pen slid up and the animal fell on its side and rolled out onto the counter in front of him.

'I can't do this,' thought Grzegorz. 'I don't know how much longer I can do this. Not for what I'm getting back from it.' The blood from the animal was washing into the gutters and into the drains. He thought about the rich scents of his grandparents' farm and the intimacy of it and of the mists coming with the cow's breath in the early morning. Of the humble pace. 'That wasn't enough,' he thought. 'That could never have been enough. We could never have kept it. Not the way the world's gone now. It was never enough anyway.' He thought of the long, flat, difficult land.

His wife had been dropped to two shifts at the factory but they still had to pay the week up front to keep the places in childcare that the agency organised.

It's over-subscribed, they said. You can't pick and choose. He was working all the time he could. 'I have to get ahead,' he thought. 'I just have to get my nose ahead then we can move on to the next step. We can get out of the shared house and have some room of our own.'

Around him, as the carcass disappeared, he could hear the men sharpening their knives. Then he heard the metal scrape and clang, and another animal went into the kill pen.

Hold steered the boat in to the quay and

the man was there waiting for him. The group of seagulls that had followed him in stopped at the harbour mouth as if there was some line there, invisible. He could feel the boat surf a little in the swell into the harbour mouth.

There were a few people walking about and you could hear the bigger traffic going past on the road even over the engine of the boat. It tocked and splashed as he slowed it up and the smell of it came to him as he cranked the propeller into reverse to stop the boat and then idled it and threw up the rope-line to the man.

'How's the sea?' said the man. He knew he didn't know his own boat. His ownership was of the idea of the boat.

Hold looked up at him. 'Getting up a little.' The man was on the quay wrapping the rope around the iron cleat.

'Tomorrow?' said the man.

He stood up from the rope. There were a few people stopped on the quay looking down into the boat at the coiled lines and the bounty of fish and at the spider crabs and the one big lobster.

The man was looking down into the boat at the boxes of fish. They were so fresh they hadn't started to lose their colour yet and in the light the fish were very fine things, and there was something somehow religious about them.

'It's your boat,' Hold said up.

'You're in it,' said the man.

Hold looked out at the sea rising slightly in a swell. 'I'm happy to take her out tomorrow.'

They'd loaded the fish up onto the quay and the man had gone into the hotel there and the restaurant manager had come out with him and chosen the fish he wanted. It was a public act and it was a very good advert for the hotel to the few early tourists. In the summer, the tourists were bolder and would gather like gulls and they would sell direct to them with their licence, setting the scales up on the quay wall.

The manager took the fish and the lobster and then they discussed something and he gave the man cash

33

and the man wrote it down in a duplicate book and gave a copy to the manager. Then he counted off the percentage of the money and added the fee to it and wrote it down and gave it to Hold.

'I took some fillets,' Hold said. He was very clear like that.

'Fine,' said the man.

The hotel manager came out then and said 'Do you want a drink, guys?' They both declined and the restaurant manager said to Hold, 'Chance you could get some rabbits for me? 'Bout a dozen?' and Hold said he could and the manager said, 'For Friday.'

'Okay,' said Hold. 'I'll go out tonight. I'll bring some in the morning or the morning after.' He knew it was a full moon and not a good night for it but figured that over two nights even with bad shooting he could get a dozen.

Every now and then he rubbed the nub of his thumb where something he'd got under his skin was swelling into a small sore. It's a fish bone, he thought. Or perhaps something off the boat. He examined it casually and scratched at it with his other thumbnail but the skin didn't lift.

'Do you want the crab?' asked the man.

The restaurant manager looked at them and looked back at the hotel and said 'They're fiddly as hell...' And Hold said, 'They're in early. Really early this year.'

'I'll take them,' said the manager. Their meat was very sweet and of great flavour but it was work to get the meat out in terms of time. 'I'll cook them up,' the manager said.

'You can have them,' said the man, and looked at Hold as if to check it with him. Hold shrugged. He flicked with his nail at the little sore again, trying to see what it was that was under his skin. He was perturbed at the crab being in so early. Usually it was from May they came in any numbers.

Hold put the tub of spider crabs on the quay wall and then they loaded the rest of the fish into the four-by-four and poured over the fish the crushed ice that was softening in the plastic sack in the back of the vehicle. Then the man drove off with them. People were staring into the big tub of spider crabs. The crabs looked very alien there on the quay wall.

Hold unwound the rope-line and cast it down into the boat and went down the ladder, kicking off the heavy boat from the wall, and the restaurant manager came out and took the crabs to cook.

Big mullet were coming in on the tide and grazing the harbour wall and people were remarking on it.

Hold headed the boat over to her mooring and tied her up and took the fillets he had cut and his water bottle and rowed the tender over to the slipway and got out. There were mullet pecking at the slipway. Around all the motors of the boats there were little rainbowed pools of oil like liquid peacock feathers lain on the water. Hold could still taste the fish in his mouth. It was a hell of a fish this way. It made it a shame to cook it.

The waste was difficult to accept.

He thought woefully of how his grandparents would be horrified by the wasteful policies of the place, of the perfectly good meat that was thrown away here.

'This is a comfortable culture,' Grzegorz thought. 'It is a comfortable culture and a culture which doesn't have time for food which takes hours to prepare. People here can choose not to eat meat. They are actually comfortable enough to be able to say I won't eat meat.'

He thought of the feet, the cow's lips, all the slow-cooked things of his upbringing, with the better cuts being sold. He saw all these unwanted organs thrown into bins and dye tipped over them, things perfectly good to eat.

'It is not what we do in this country,' he told himself. 'There is enough here.' He thought bitterly of the useless farm back home, the place he had always imagined himself staying. Felt the dagger of his naivety in that. 'We have to move on. Get more sophisticated.'

It was criminal, but most of the farms round here

were small. Not by Polish standards, but they were small and they sold through organisations that had contracts with the big supermarkets. For most people, there was no getting away from that if they wanted to make the farm work.

When a supermarket put in a big order for something they wanted to sell on offer they got the animals they needed in and took just those parts and threw the rest of the animal away. The supermarkets, for example, would want lamb chops, so they'd extract the chops and send them on down to the packing line and the rest of the sheep would be tossed, and the dye thrown on it. Then the chops would be driven for hundreds of miles around the country.

The suppliers and the farmers would have to take the financial hit on the offer or risk losing the supermarket contract, and if any of the product was left unsold when the offer ran out, the supplier had to buy it back.

Grzegorz thought of the animals butchered in the old kitchen, the pig hanging from its sinews by the big iron hooks and his grandfather's saw cutting down through the ribs, the collected pudding of the blood, the rich, powerful smell of the fresh offal on the wood-fired stove. 'This gratefulness to an animal,' he thought, 'is what's gone here. There is a sorrow for it, as there always is, but it is without gratefulness and eventually you just go numb to it. It's the way you have to feel about crowds of people, about strangers. You can't care for them. You can't let yourself. There's too many of them.'

Much of the meat that should have been destroyed went missing. You couldn't work in that wastefulness and go home and see people eating poorly, counting their pennies. That was one thing about the house, despite the lack of ready money – they ate well. At least, they ate richly from the cuts the men could bring. Last week a whole lorry load of chops had come back. They'd gone all the way through, through the packing lines and onto the lorry and the hundreds of miles to the supermarket depot and they were rejected because the rind of fat was half a centimetre too thick. They had to be destroyed. The supervisor came out to oversee that one and they had to watch the whole lot go to waste. It was perfectly good meat.

He thought tiredly of the dressing down again. The bullying, as it was, by his line manager. 'Maybe I attract it,' he thought. 'Maybe I attract that kind of thing. They think I'm weak because I'm quiet. I'm not a city boy like them. I never learnt to be aggressive like that.'

He looked up at his wife. She was shushing the baby in this kind of worn out way, the other people in the kitchen moving round her. He was losing hope, he could feel that. He could feel the energy that came with that first, excited belief disappearing. And she seemed to be disappearing with it.

At first, there had been something alive in the snatched, silenced embraces they had stolen in the crowded house. This fresh sense of newness about everything. Now they were too tired, too ashamed, too aware of the eleven other beds in the room, the baby in the basket by their bed. He thought of the farm, his own childhood. Whatever it lacked, of the richness of the space. 'To bring a baby up here, in this,' he thought.

He pushed the food around his plate, bumped and jostled as others cooked and ate in the small kitchen.

He could see out of the window the big graffiti saying Polish out, and could hear his wife chuck to the baby. He felt this loss of her happening.

'*Wciąż się kłócimy*,' he thought. We are always quarrelling now.

He could feel the drudgery come round him the way it had become at home, as if it was something physical that could happen to you. The automaticness to just get through.

'It doesn't change,' he thought. 'Life stays the same, relatively. Unless you get one big chance to get yourself ahead, properly ahead, then it just stays the same.'

It was getting enough to make the next step, that's all it was. They put what they could away, but it was haemorrhaging, with what everything cost here. It was all relative. He believed it was just the next step, then he could change everything.

39

'I didn't expect to be here for so long,' he thought. He meant the house. He looked at his wife. He could see she looked visibly older.

Hold drove the old van back.

There was the sense that the van somehow hung together around him. The repairs Hold had made himself were all over and there were many patches of gaffer tape spread over the van like a kid that had come off their bike. He was never someone who had craved great amounts of money but it was tiring to not be able to afford simple things anytime, like a pair of new boots, or to have the money just to fix up the van.

Of course, there was always the dream of a fortune, just to make everything safe and fix up the place, but it was not a wistfulness in him. But now came this. This need for big money, or the house would go.

He pulled up by the caravan and got out and then rethought and leant back in to pick up the fillets from the front seat, as the sun warmed in through the windscreen. He took the fillets and went into his caravan and put them in the paper in the fridge and he looked down at some of the stray scales still on his hands and went into the shower.

*

The house had been Danny's grandparents', and as they had aged they had sold off the land and the bungalow they had built on it but had kept the old house. For the first ten years of their life, the place had been their universe, Danny and his, and Danny had been crushed by the selling of it. For a child, it was not possible that things could not be permanent. With the money from selling off the land his grandparents had rented a small place in the village, and the old house decayed on the plot. The dream in the family was that one day they could rebuild it and move into it in a kind of reclamation, and it had been Danny's great hope that he would be able to do this.

Danny was a dreamer. That is not to say he was not a determined man, but he was a man who set up great dream-like things all the time and had this refusal to accept the unlikeliness of them. Often in the sight of the big idea, Danny would overlook the processional steps you needed, the simple things to get somewhere. There was something childlike in this, but he had a great way of bringing you with him, so even when you knew the end was not possible you would get caught up in the getting there. It was a very contagious thing. There was something in his belief that was very contagious and made you wish you didn't have an idea of reality sometimes. But the house was not an impossibility. The house just needed the hours spent, the materials gathered, the skills applied.

*

Hold came out of the shower and stood in the steam that roiled out of the small shower room and watched the motes of moisture catch the incoming light. Through the window he could see the house and there was, every time he looked at it, this recall of the promise he'd made. This unmovable, stone-built thing of it.

'Finish it for him. Finish it for Jake.' Hold had sat by the bed, his wasting friend seeming to desiccate before him, and him hardly able to take in the actuality of it.

He looked now at the way some of the limed whitewash was lifting, aged, off the wallstones and thought of his friend's skin seeming to dry off, to flake away as he lay there. He looked out and saw that the stray cat had come to sit on the van bonnet for the dissolving warmth of the engine. He was always taking in strays; he preferred it to the responsibility of ownership.

'I want to give him something to belong to,' said Danny.

'I'll do that,' Hold said. 'I'll do that thing.'

Since then, any money he had he put into the things he needed for the house, and it was coming, bit by bit. He had long resolved for it to be a far off thing to achieve, but now had come the bombshell. Danny's sister wanted her share of the money from the place.

It was like she'd held out while Danny was alive, swayed by his promises that he'd find the money to buy her out. Then had come her divorce, and then Danny had gone. She needed the money, now. It was like this giant, final, impassable wall.

Hold had tried everything he could. He had submitted a business plan to the bank himself, for a boat of his own, the likely return after three and five years, all as it said in the book he'd bought. He had been cautious and harsh with the plan but the figures still looked good, but the bank had simply refused. You have nothing. We can't lend with that risk.

His idea had been to borrow the money for the start-up but to siphon some off and arrange to buy her out bit by bit, as the money came in. But Cara wouldn't consider it. It was enough for her to know he had worked on the house for Jake. All these things he did were for Jake, they both had to believe that. It was academic anyway. He couldn't raise the money.

He took a sliver off one of the fillets and took it outside and gave the sliver to the stray. He had to choke down this moment of sudden anger at knowing that the house was going to slip away because of the one thing he could not compete on, money, and that this castle they'd played inside would be knocked down and rebuilt and sold off to the highest bidder, almost certainly as a second home. He saw the two of them inside, juvenile, the dangerous fires they had lit

43

there in secret, the things they'd invented with great weaponry value hidden there, the plans they'd made, the first girlfriends they had brought there.

I could change it, if I had just once chance, he thought. If just one chance came along. He watched the cat eat the fillet, half bolt it, the way the opportunist has to take their chance. He felt this great draw, this need to go to them, and he knew that taking the fillets was just yet another excuse, but there was a magnetism working, as if he was sucked into the great void of his friend at this time. It was like he felt the need to apologise for his failure to keep the house, but could not find the words. In this sudden failure there was some sort of need to be close to them, as if he wanted some sort of forgiveness from Danny.

'I'll take the fillets along,' he thought. 'I'll put out the shore nets. I could do with the space of the beach.'

The baby was being fed when the row broke out and he started to scream immediately when their voices went up and the other boy, too, started to cry. Started to cry just with the sheer completeness of everyone's upset, his baby brother wailing, his mother covering herself angrily and reddening and launching into one of those shapeless female arguments that is just a letting go of all the exhausting little frustrations.

44

And his father just emitting this great, weary uselessness at everything, as if it all fell on him, looking like he was taking in her words like they were something foul he had in his mouth and was deciding on whether to spit up.

They can be vicious in argument, women, and she sliced into him over and over, and all his weaknesses that he had offered up to her, in some great amnesty of masculinity, that he had offered her as signs of his true scale as nothing more than a simple man, she sliced at and tore into. And his children yelled, as if they watched this flaying of their father.

He had not seen her like this before. He realised they had never really argued, and all of this was pouring out of her. She even looked ugly to him, the way she was then.

'You promised things,' she said. 'I left everything behind. You promised we would have things.'

He felt all the weight of that.

'You promised things.'

He knocked and came in through the porch, taking off his shoes, and went through to the kitchen and put the fillets in their newspaper down on the side and she met him in almost a sedate way. When Hold had been on the sea, he smelled of Danny to her

45

and it was difficult for her not to react at that so she quite often had this distant thing about her. She was just making tea and reached down another cup automatically and put in a teabag and poured on the still boiled water from the kettle that puffed steam up into the underside of the hanging unit, and took up her own cup and held it and blew over it and looked at the parcel on the worktop.

'Present,' said Hold.

Cara took out the teabag and squeezed it against the side of the cup and lifted it out to the little plastic food tray she had for compost to throw on the border. She bent for the milk from the fridge and he watched deliberately, instead, the steam come off the teabag and curl up amongst the broken eggshells and peelings there like some far away sign. Like the engine smoking across the top of the boat.

She put in the milk and passed him the cup and he looked down at the fillets on the side, looking at the newspaper they were wrapped in, the black print furring out from itself, leaving some chromatogram-like aura around the words.

'Bass,' he said, and she nodded. Her sleeves were rolled up, like she'd been doing kitchen work and hadn't had time to change her clothes. Hold looked at the way she was dressed in the respectable clothes and said, 'How was the bank?'

She gave the slightest shake of her head.

46

He put the tea down and opened a cupboard, mainly so she couldn't see the flash of anger on his face.

'How was the sea today?' she said to him. He was going through the cupboards like the house was his own.

'She's getting up. Not so soon, though. Be a few days.'

'Thanks for the fish.'

'It's good fish,' he said. He was thinking of the house, and how he had promised Danny he would have it for the boy. 'Where's he at?'

'He's out on his bike.' There was a moment of space. They both noticed at the same time and were uncomfortable with it.

'Are you looking for biscuits?'

'It's fine.'

She looked apologetic that there were no biscuits. Like she had let him down. There was no play. None of the bantered flirting there used to be, while Danny was still with her; none of the soft edgemanship they both harmlessly enjoyed, like dogs chasing the same ball in a park. None of what was just gentle rhythmic chemistry, a safe peacefulness to it when Danny was alive and could watch it, and valued it in some way as this great reassurance of his choice in her that his friend could have this intentless thing with her.

He looked down at the sore welling on his thumb.

It was one of those small things. He picked at it.

'Do you have a needle?' he asked.

Cara took his hand and looked at it. 'It's not ready yet. You'll just dig into yourself. Leave it. It will lift.'

Hold nodded at her.

'You should let me take him out soon,' he said. And she nearly called him Danny but then she said, 'Holden, he's too young. And it's a school night.'

They sipped their tea a while.

'You've got the nets out?'

'I've just set them.'

He had gone from the quay and driven over to the beach and taken the net over his shoulder out along the shore in the tough old spoil bag. It made sense if he was coming for rabbits on the cliff that night to have some point to aim for and work down to, but more than this physical excuse it was that something went from him on the beach.

Danny's death had become a great thing, and a point of time from which all things seemed to be measured. Hold felt very strongly the responsibility to create some new point for things to come from, some positive beginning point like the birth of a child to a couple. He had a vision of them all sitting on a bench in the sunshine outside the finished house. He felt as if he needed some sign to have that purpose. He felt greatly that a renewed energy was needed, and that

48

perhaps from this positive thing, in this good momentum, it would not be the betrayal to go with her as it would be from hurt, in this space of damage. If it grew out of something good and new they had built for themselves and wasn't simply them falling into the space that Danny's death had created.

The bass fish side to side, zigzagging for things disturbed along the breaking lip of the inward tide, so the gill net is laid across the beach, right-angled to the sea over the uncovered pools to catch them as they follow in the tide. Once they choose a course, if the net is there, they hit it.

In the rushing water, the nylon mesh of the net would be invisible to the fish and Hold could imagine them striking the net, that first moment of bloody confusion and the increased power to swim on, driving them further into the mesh, the scales shed in the water, the line fitting fatally behind their gills. He pushed the thought away.

As he had left the beach the sun was starting to bleed out into the evening. The warmth hadn't come into things yet and he knew it would be a cool night. Again, the peregrine had come off the cliffs and for a while circled over him as he lay the net, in witness, the hunter come to watch the hunter. There was a real definition to the thing against the thinning evening light.

*

'You should come out again. You and Jake.'

And he remembered then, in full detail, her shoulders, bare, the thin open shirt licking out in the wind, the surprise freckles on her shoulders seeming to flush then merge under the sun, like drops of something onto clean cloth; and Danny drove the boat head on to the waves and got her jumping, with the childishness over her face at the enjoyment of it; and Danny, so proud. And it seemed like Hold had only understood that word proud then for the first time. That pride in his friend. And Hold knew that he would have a care for this girl that was like that close care for a friend's child, and that she was partly his to look after.

And she remembered him. This friend of Danny's with his strange meaning name. How he was more methodical and quiet than Danny, and less flashy. And how he brought up the fish, and helped her with the rod when she caught her first string of mackerel and they came wheeling and flapping into the boat and she was screaming and laughing and seeing the broad proud smile of her man. But how Hold had taken the rod without taking it off her and brought in the line and flicked off the mackerel with some calm respect and sense of his own place that she felt this richness of, as Danny steered the boat idling through the water. And she had felt from this man she was meeting for the first time great patience and great solidity and some great power of decision that made her feel very

50

safe around him, as if she knew he would never alter his mind about her. And it made her love Danny more, that he had a friend like this.

And that same image had balled at them, then, in that one phrase he had said. That she should come out. And they had understood, together, that at all costs there must be no private space. Not to walk too close to the edge of the cliff.

'Will you do the window for me?' she asked.

'Sure,' he said. 'You think it was kids?'

She nodded. She felt the need to explain. 'I still can't go in there.'

'It's fine,' he said.

He went into the shed and put the

padlock with the key still in it down on the shelf by the broken window. Glass had gone over the shelf and onto the floor and Holden could see the tarmac-covered chipping that had come through the window.

Dust was on the other window panels and looked scaly in the last of the sun. At the window corners the sun caught in the spider webs, vaguely bluish.

Hold picked up the chipping and threw it from the door and brushed off the glass splinters from the window shelf.

He could feel Danny's presence here. Or the absence

of him that he could usually avoid.

The dust had settled quickly over the place. 'I know how it will go. She will do her best to carry on, to stay positive. But this will come down on her, this dust. This tiredness and lack of use. And then she'll be dry and worn out and beaten.' He felt great pain at knowing this with such certainty.

'I should have been firmer,' he said to himself. 'I should have insisted he got it checked out. The one time I didn't push, that I took a step back. It was part of his character too,' thought Hold. 'To bury his head in the sand. Not face responsibility. But he should have got it looked at. I should have pushed him harder.'

He tipped one tub of screws into another to empty a tub and put into it the broken glass and squatted and pecked up the larger fragments from the floor.

The rods and tools were around the walls.

He went through a pile of wood and picked out some hardboard and took down a saw from a nail and found in the rack of small tools a measuring tape.

He cut the piece to the size of the window panel, measuring with the rusted tape and marking his measures with a nail, and he set the cut piece into the hole and pinned it up.

'This is not good, us both like this,' he said, and pushed that out from his mind. 'This?' he asked himself. 'There isn't a this.'

He gave one of the uprights an absent push, as if

to see that the shed had solidity, and perhaps in some way in that act he was testing his own strength.

I wonder if Jake comes in here. I wonder if he comes in here to his father's things. I wonder if he remembers. I wonder if he knows where the key is and comes secretly in here and feels okay.

Hold looked at the things. Such strange refuse we leave. In the corner, the hexagons of an old wasps' nest, husks of paper.

He looked at the old bait fridge, all pitted and measled with rust, and looked in it and seeing it empty found the plug and unplugged it.

He picked up the old metal detector and switched it on to see if it worked and waved it about and it sang shrilly at the metal but it was somehow as if it was Danny the machine detected.

'Hey, Danny,' he said. And there was thirty years in it, and all the three years of his absence.

He took the metal detector with him, and locked up the shed.

'Why don't you stay for supper?'
she said.

'I have the nets out.'

'Doesn't stop you eating supper,' Cara said.

'Are you shooting tonight?' asked the kid.

'No, Jake,' said his mother, not as the answer, just

to stop him before he started. But he had his father's irresistible capacity.

'Yeah, I'm shooting tonight.'

He felt Cara look at him. 'It won't be such a good night,' he said to put the boy off. 'Too much moon. That's good for the nets though.' He was trying to feed the boy little knowledges always.

'Something draws them. I don't know what it is. But something draws them up in that moon.'

The kid was looking at him. He was ignoring the mysterious thing Hold was doing. 'Why isn't it good for shooting?' It was all about the gun. It was like he didn't want to know about the fish.

'If you're staying, that's it with the talk,' Cara said.

They took the tripe home in a black bin sack. On the women's orders they took it into the garden and hung it like some great shroud and then washed the clinging gouts of cud and the stomach liquids off then they carried it inside like some foul painter's sheet and butchered it up on the table.

The place stank for weeks with the intestinal, unmistakable odour of the tripe cooking but it was good solid food. It had this strange effect on the house, like the bringing home of a big fish, and Grzegorz felt

54

a type of pride. All the time, they brought back what they could without morally resorting in their minds to stealing. It was just the left over stuff, the things gone to waste, the heavy, clubby bones of beef that they put into the *flaczki*, the rich tripe soup.

There was the odour, though, the odour that stuck about the house as if it had crept into the fabrics of the place and mixed up with the sharp permanent smell of the vinegar from always pickling vegetables, the smells of the habit of storage, of having to make it through winter. To Grzegorz, it was the smell of poorness, of home. Of the leaden humbleness of his grandparents. Of his own naivety to think that he could live that way, with that little, in the world as it was now.

He thought of the farm. 'It would not be possible,' he thought. 'We've seen other things now, we want other things. It would never have been possible to stay there.'

One by one the tiny farms, most of them less than ten acres, had folded in. At first, it was like watching candles guttering out; but then, with the big European supermarkets moving into the town suburbs with their cheaper prices, the farms just seemed to be snuffed, one by one, by this unbeatable instrument of economy wielded at arms' length. 'We are a poor people, we have to buy the cheapest,' thought Grzegorz. 'You couldn't expect people to fight them.' He thought bitterly of the old timber house, the warm, sweet smell of animals, the constant smell of food cooking, like now, food with this lingering odour.

The government were trying to force the farms to consolidate, trying to ball them all up and remould them into bigger, more competitive units so they could feasibly ask for European grants. But the people involved were balled up in the wax of these policies. Now the foreigners were coming in and buying up vast tracts of land that cost them next to nothing, turning them into holiday resorts and golf courses. 'We could never have stayed,' he told himself. These farms, some two million or so of them, had survived the Russians, the Germans and Communism but could not beat this simple mathematical annihilation, this new invasion of wealthy outsiders. He knew in his heart, with a stench of guilt, that they could never have taken on the farm anyway, that it was an illusion, that it was better the choice had been crushed.

'We want more now,' said Grzegorz. 'We're not so simple. We can't be happy living the old way any more. It is better to be here. Poland can rot.'

On the stove, the tripe boiled, and the stench went through the house.

He watched her cook. She had the apron on and doubled at the waist with the cord around it and her collar stayed off her shoulders and he saw the surprise freckles there, starting just on her shoulders. He stopped himself. He had fantasised about her a lot when Danny was alive but after he died had stopped himself, refused to let himself, as if it was some kind of bigger betrayal.

He was drinking one of the beers she always kept in the fridge for him and could hear in the next room Jake going round with the metal detector finding the metal things he had hidden about.

He watched Cara put the fillets into the butter in the pan and they arched slightly as the skin burned, and relaxed again. She levered them over and he looked at the beautiful netted skin of the fish, emphasised in its burning.

She stooped down and opened the oven and flicked her hair over her ear and with the oven gloves shook up the tray of oven chips and turned the tray of the loose chips round and slid it back in and shut the oven again. When she turned the fish over once more the meat was bright white.

Hold went through and helped Jake clear up the metal things all around and ready the table and she brought the plates through with the fish on and put the chips and the peas on the table. Looking at the fish, Hold had this bizarre thing that it was some white affinity that brought the fish to the moon. A sense of light.

The metal detector was in the corner and needed to be cleaned up after all the time in the shed and Hold decided he would take it and clean it.

He remembered the time Danny had hidden things about the garden for the boy, all sorts of metal objects, planting them under stones, burying them at the foot of the hedgerow. The way Danny could bring a sense of adventure into something.

The boy was younger then and every time he found something he came running to them. The find of the day had been the brooch. It was a beautiful, intricate and damaged thing. The boy gave it to his mum.

'That's pretty cool,' Hold had said.

'I didn't put that there,' said Danny secretively. He had this massive, victorious wide grin.

The boy noticed Hold looking at the instrument.

'We could go treasure hunting,' said the boy, and Hold looked thoughtfully at him.

'Maybe there's treasure on the beach.'

'Maybe there is,' said Hold. 'Maybe there's ambergris.'

The word had this kind of magic sense to it.

'What's ambergris?' asked the boy.

Jake was picking at the chips with his hands and his mother gave him a look which stopped him.

'Ambergris?' said Hold. The boy was looking at him. He remembered Danny's newspaper cutting, the way he had waved it with this intent belief they could find some, that it would fall to them. More, that he lived always with this chorus behind him, 'what if?', always 'what if?'

'It's whale sick,' said Hold. The boy eew-ed and laughed and did not believe him and thought he was starting one of those games grown-ups do.

'It's whale sick and it smells of cow poo. Cow poo and perfume. Like a farm girl on a night out.' The boy was delighted.

Cara was trying to be stern but was smiling and warm at seeing the boy laugh. Men bring an irreverence, she thought. It's good to have that. She looked at Hold ladling mayonnaise onto his plate and missed the capableness and the solidity that can be in a man's hands.

'It's something very rare,' said Hold, getting serious. 'It's grey, ish, and it stinks and a piece the size of your plate is worth more than a new car.'

The boy's eyes went cartoon wide. 'No way,' he said.

'Look it up,' Holden said. 'Maybe there's some on the beach.' He thought of Danny's chorus: never rule out maybe. What if? What if, really? What would he do for the chance to be able to lift all this, lift her and the boy off the tracks they were stuck on?

Cara looked at him. Sometimes she felt as if she had one half of a man and under her clothes she could feel her body going to waste. It was he who had drawn the line. She would never hold it against

59

him if he loved her. It was his standing off that was difficult to take.

After supper he said 'I could take him with me tonight,' and she had said 'No.' The boy was washing up and the industrious clattering came from the kitchen. Hold was toying with the salt grinder, making rings of salt on the tablecloth and pushing them into shapes with his fingers.

'He's old enough now,' Hold said. He put the salt grinder down. 'He wouldn't shoot. He'd just walk with me. It might even put him off, seeing it. It does some people. He's not going to let go of it otherwise.'

Cara looked at him. 'It's a school-night.'

'Most of the kids will be up on their computers.'

'Not mine.' She was quiet.

'He won't let it go, you know.'

She could feel very much that it was Hold who wanted the boy to go with him, and she waited for a long time. She felt sometimes that she should try to make the decisions Danny would have made, and not just her own. To be fairer to the boy. And she knew that she was out of her depth trying to bring up a boy and give him all the leeway the things he would want would take. She had a great urge to hold Danny at the thought of the boy's growing up, and in a split second she saw his broadening, and the ropes and sinews come into his arms and legs and the coming angularity of him. I need help with all this, she felt. It's too much, all these decisions on my own.

'How long will you be out?' she asked him.

'I could go out earlier, for an hour or two with him, and bring him back. There won't be much anyway. I could drive down for the nets after.'

'And he won't shoot?'

'He'll just walk with me, and see it.' He played with the sore atop his thumb, looking down to see if he could tell what was under it.

Cara stood up and called the boy and he came through. 'Sit down,' she said.

He was worried underneath being told to sit down. This is how it had come. There was always that doubt after that, his emotions all curled up like a cat, waiting to react to the huge, incomprehensible news. He knew it was stupid to feel it, but he couldn't help it coming. Hold knew it, recognised it.

She told him that if he went to bed now, and got some sleep, he could go shooting tonight. Just for a few hours. Then she went out and finished the clearing up.

Danny had died without any cover.

In this, there was a crippling lack of responsibility and Hold had had a great anger at his friend, and Cara had understood in those brief angry, bereft moments when he could not help her seeing that it had always been that way, and that it was he who had always exercised the practicalities, the safeties for what they did. The pot of water when they lit fires, the flares for the boat, calling the coastguard in advance when they went out on the boat for the night. Danny had never considered that things could go wrong, turn for the worst. Or if he had, he buried his head from them. It was what was engaging about him, but it worked only with the balancing responsibility Hold took.

Hold had sold the boat, and she had seen the great wrench of that as if someone had lifted a part of him away. She knew it was their dream between them, a few years on to work the boat and live by fishing and she could never erase the way his face looked when it went. The humble money from that had got her through the immediate costs and with her work she could just clear the mortgage. But there was nothing over. There was enough value in the old house to set them up, but she couldn't consider that with the way Danny had been about it, with the way Hold had taken on the responsibility of it. Sometimes she saw it as this great weight that was just dragging them all down, keeping Hold in Danny's shadow, a locked up store of money, a constant reminder of the past she wished inside she could just break away from, a millstone dragging them always into the great sea of his absence.

She wanted to be let go. She could not bear the not being there of him and was confused by the emotions that were growing in her that seemed a betrayal of this great feeling.

'It's just not possible,' the bank had said, and she had felt this internal, secret relief, that the house would go. She understood the responsibility Hold felt, understood how it felt for someone to invest their dreams in you the way Danny did. How that made you feel valuable and needed in a way that was difficult to get free from. But Hold too was a confusion to her now, a weight on her moving on. She did not know whether it was love because that thing seemed too fragile for her now but she had fallen in great care with him. It was just another fact. Another little awareness that made itself known to her, awareness which made her desperate, so she could feel small hatreds of herself growing inside, things she tried to accept or cocoon so they did not seep through her and bitter everything.

She felt, despite this great want to be around him, that it was unfair of him to be there. Sometimes she wanted to orchestrate something that would finalise it, that he could not forgive himself for. She thought of his hands on her, how her body missed touch.

Hold me, or let me go, let us go. It's stifling you bringing him back into our life every time.

Hold came back about eleven and took the key from the nail in the porch and let himself in and put the stuff he had got together for the boy on the floor and went through to the kitchen and turned on the kettle to fill up the flasks.

She said she'd be in bed. 'You wake him. Make it a man thing,' she said. 'Just bring him back.' That sentence was so loaded that it went right through Holden when she said it. There was nothing strong enough he could say to it.

He put boiled water in the flasks to warm them and went to the boy's room. Jake was sleeping. He'd got his penknife and a first aid kit out by his bed and had pulled green and camouflage clothes out from his drawers.

Hold looked down at the boy and shook him gently and said his name. He felt a strange sense of fathership, beyond his own flesh and blood. The boy looked perturbed in his sleep. Because you couldn't see the old-looking eyes the boy had, from what he'd been through, he looked much younger sleeping. The boy had her eyes, and without them Hold could see Danny very clearly in the boy.

He shook Jake again but he didn't wake. It was as if he was concentrating on sleep. And seeing him sleeping that way, Hold suddenly had no desire to wake him. As if he acknowledged that the boy wasn't ready for this yet. That things should wait.

He took the piece of shale he'd taken from the beach and put it down on the boy's cabinet. It was rhomboid, smoothed at the corners, and the three clear crystals of fool's gold lay in a line across it, like three small dice part way through a roll.

He knew the boy was too old for it now, and would know it was worthless. But maybe he would play along. It's what we feel something is that makes it important. In a fire, someone might grab the most worthless thing, a smooth pebble, a seashell, a dried old rose if their lover had given it to them. If they still had the energy to believe. It's what a thing is capable of being that matters.

He looked at the boy for an odd while, then went out of the room.

He left the house and put the key through the door and got in the van. 'I should have gone to her and told her that the boy wasn't coming out with me,' he said inside himself. 'She'll work it out.' There was no way he could have gone into that room, and sometimes he knew that it was part cowardice at the responsibility he would have to take on then. It might be different if he had something that she could make a choice for. If the house was done. I could never walk into that thing Danny has put around them, this bungalow, his place, he thought. He could not imagine himself existing in his friend's space, not like that.

65

She heard him go and knew he had not taken the boy. And she had a strong image of him then, leaning over and helping her pull in the line, and not taking the rod off her. And then she felt this great god damned confusion over him.

He parked up the van and switched off the lights and the lights seemed to take a brief moment to go out. He knew she was right that the boy was too young to be with him for this but he also knew it was the sometimes female thing of not wanting your child to play with guns. Not from a sense of pacifism, but for the sense of responsibility it involved, and the growing up it represented. I should take the boy out in the day and shoot some clays, show him the danger of this thing first, he thought. There was a relief that the boy was not with him and he would not have to explain everything he did, but there was also the sense of responsibility to him; and there had come a strange sense in him, stronger as he had grown older, that the things he knew should be passed on, the sense that otherwise there was no point in things, and part of his encouragement of the boy was to give himself a chance of this.

He poured a coffee out of the flask and set the cup down on the dashboard and watched the heat steam up the windscreen by the cup. Below was the crush and swell of the tide going out and he could sense it in the rich and fertile moonlight. There was really a sense of being on the edge here.

Further north, the bay curved round and you could see the lights of towns, but before him was the sea with just the few lights of the scallop boats out. It gave the sense of being at the edge of an element. It was like a limit, that water, and Hold felt it would be impossible for him to move away from it. It was as if he needed the sense of this limit somehow, the great, wide humbling space of it. If she moves away, I don't think I'll be able to follow, he thought.

He got out of the van and shook out the coffee cup and screwed it back onto the flask and put it in the driver's doorwell and the van was very white in the moonlight. He looked up at the moon for a while, more because it was impossible not to look up at it, somehow. Don't think about all the other stuff now, he said. Put it away. It's what you do this for.

He opened the back and took out the gun from its case and checked it over with this careful, rhythmic habit. He tapped the light in the van back as it went out briefly and it came back on with a small buzz and he looked at the bright moon again and knew it would mean the rabbits would see him. Then he put the gun back in the case and checked that the silencer was with him and put the loose bullets in his left coat pocket and picked up the game bag with a small jerk

67

to hear that the knife and the scales were in it amongst the plastic bags he kept for the fish.

He went round to shut the driver's door and flicked down the sun visor and checked that in the pocket band was the five pound note he was paid to keep the vermin down each year and that he kept from superstition – though he'd say he wasn't a superstitious man.

In this ritual, he could feel this first slight thing come up in him and some tone in his blood and he kept it down with this patient procedure. It was a thing peculiar only to the gun and having the gun near him and he associated it in his mind with the flavour the smell of the rifle made in his mouth. There was the metal smell of the barrel and the gun oil and casings and the brief taste of foil in his mouth so even the iron and oil of the van seemed amplified, and in this Pavlovian thing he felt his nostrils flare slightly and the oxygen feel better and more useful in his head. For him, there was a very right thing in all this and something very old. It was this rightness of it, not any love of killing or feel of sport, that was his reason for doing it, and in the focus of doing it he felt his other worries begin to leave him.

He took the lamp and checked it on and off and said in his head to remember to put it on charge in the morning. Then he shut the van and he opened the gate with the bag and the gun on his shoulder and went out onto the low slope at the top of the cliffs.

It was in that rich and very fertile moonlight that he went on, following the sheep track to the fence that demarked the land he was paid to shoot over. And though he could see the gathering banks of cloud shift in from the south, in that moonlight he knew that there would be less chance of rabbits, but that the huge, social power of that moon would draw in the fish way up the beach inside the big tide, and that if the fish were there, they would go into the net.

He swapped the bullets from the left pocket of his coat to his right in the final stage of his ritual and hung the game bag on the fence by the stile when he'd climbed over, with the split blue polythene pipe over the barbed wire looking almost white in that moon.

He took out the gun and checked it rhythmically again and checked the barrel and screwed on the silencer and rested it against the stile and folded up the gun bag and pushed it into the game bag and clipped up the straps. Then he took up his things and went on into the wind, the breeze taking the smell of him and of his metal and bags back behind him, and herding the sounds of him off.

Below, the tide pounded with some sense of potential power contained, crushed languidly onto the beach. And though it hardly felt like anything, the breeze of that changing tide sounded heavier than it was, and he knew that where the rabbits would be, at the edge of the cliffs, it would be sloughing through the thorn, and in its loudness there would be cover for any noise he made.

He knew the rabbits would see him in the moonlight and he stopped high up the slope and shaded the rifle from glinting in the moon with his arm and looked up towards the thin approaching cloud, the stars pendant in the night. Of the few star constellations that he knew, he could see Orion and felt for it some affinity, this son of the sea god, the hunter again to the hunter witness.

When he drew his own constellations, as he had done as a child, it was a lobster he made out in these stars. If he had known that one of those stars was called Cara, he might have read into that something mysterious and read it as a message, or some sign. But he did not know, for all the years he had been looking at it and looking at her.

Cara, he thought. He had this fear inside that when the house was gone she might move away, that perhaps it was only this physical anchor which kept her here. He had the sense of this as if it was a knowledge, and something that was bound to happen. I need them to be able to give to, he thought. I couldn't formalise it though. I need to be free to give. Feed the stray cat. If it gets to be something, they will expect reliability from me. I can't face that dependence. I can't face the responsibility of that.

If I had one chance, he thought. One chance then

I could change it round.

He squatted before some gorse to break up his shape and could see from there, some hundred yards before him, the shape of the rabbits and picked them out from the molehills and humps of grass and easily when they moved by their moonlit tails. And they lopped and ate at the edge of the gorse and every now and then inquired into the night air as they finished the grass in their mouths with their rhythmic, vital chewing.

He tried to push the thoughts from his mind, the other ghosts of distraction. This is why he came here, this is why he did this: to reach some space. To push everything else from his mind.

A few fields over he could hear the bleats of the newly turned out lambs, calling for their mothers in the night, and the maternal patience in the answering mearghhs. The bad rain had kept off and it had been a good year for the lambs so far as the wet on their backs could bring them down very quickly. Somewhere, the plaintive call of a fox.

He knew this place well now. The field he was in was not farmed hard and it was scattered with stands of blackthorn and gorse, and sprawling piles of bramble. Everything had a bonsai quality to it, a denseness brought on by the constant, stunting grazing, the tough salt wind.

*

The first time he ever shot rabbits he was alone and it was with a shotgun and he had been looking for a long time with this growing sense he did not know how to do what he was doing. Then there were two in the top of the last field he came to. He instantly crouched. He could feel his heartbeat.

The field gently curved in the middle and the rabbits were beyond the crest some way on the downward slope. The field had been ploughed and rolled and new shoots of barley were coming through in it. It was some hundred metres to the rabbits.

He held the gun in one hand and went almost crab-like on his bent legs and outstretched other arm, keeping his head low and trying to gauge where he reached the crest of the slope. The field was the highest part of the farmland and the view from it could take your breath sometimes. The barley shoots were all shaking in the breeze.

He had stopped for a while and had no idea what to do. He could see just above the crest and the two rabbits were between the rows of barley going from shoot to shoot. His heart was beating unreasonably and there was something in the feel and smell of the damp warm soil under his hands and the moisture from the earth coming through his trousers as he knelt that put him back to childhood. Doing this thing was a very new thing for him and he had no knowledge of what would happen next and in this the expectancy was very pure like a child's.

Crouched as he was, he could hear the barley shoots rattle in the breeze. He had no idea what to do. As soon as he moved, the rabbits would go. There was a reason for shooting the rabbits. He wanted to cook them and he wanted that very much after hearing the old guy in the pub talk of the rabbit trains they used to send full of meat to London in the war; how no one seemed to use the things around them any more. It was a responsibility he wanted to take. He clicked off the safety.

When he stood up, the rabbits ran. What happened was very quick, but it had never left him. He shot the furthest one and it balled into the ground and went still and then he shot the second one mid-leap and it hit the soil and squealed and bucked into the air and he watched it as it hit the ground and volleyed again horribly into the air over and over, writhing and leaping down the field as if it was on a string held by some sick god, the way we dangle a toy for a cat. And he cracked open the gun and shook as he rushed for more cartridges walking almost hypnotised towards the rabbit, and he swallowed in the horror of it with some bizarre pragmatism he did not know he had.

And then the rabbit was on the ground and kicked up scuffs of soil it loosened as it fought and he levelled the gun and just held it there, sick with his own heartbeat, not knowing whether to fire or not, then the rabbit went still. The space around it was smashed and all the barley shoots were ripped out.

He collected the two rabbits and took them down and the old farmer showed him how to skin them and he never told anyone about the puppet rabbit.

He hoped very much when he shot again that it would not reoccur, and he had never again managed to hit two things with each barrel in succession like that. He was young and it had come to him as another big lesson in responsibility, but there was a relief in it. He understood it as a different type of responsibility.

It was an outward symbol of the capacity to take liability. It seemed manly, and yet it was a responsibility which ended with the result of one quick action. There was not the responsibility that comes with love or ambition, of having to maintain the determination and energy towards the thing you chose to achieve. The thing or person. This responsibility ended with the death you had decided to mete out. You didn't have to risk watching the ideal decay.

Hold put the head torch on and walked down the field and stopped, sensing the rabbits scutter and shift ahead of him, seeing him first in the moonlight. He flicked on the lamp and scanned the space in front in a slow, sweeping arc and the rabbits looked back at him, their misunderstanding eyeshine reflected back in pinkish discs.

The bullet spat through the silencer and in the scope he saw the rabbit turn over and shake and die, its mouth still working for a second, then its back leg kicking automatically out in the final statement of its instinct like some unwound spring, and he lowered the scope and switched off the beam so as not to see the final parts of its life shudder out of it. He went over the tide times in his mind and worked out how long he had to work his way down to the nets on the beach.

You could leave the nets there and let them be exposed but there was always the chance that something would get into them if you had any fish. There wouldn't be birds in the night, not before dawn, but a fox would go down there, and even a polecat, or otter, which they said were getting stronger again and would follow the freshwater streams down to the shore and hunt there. On the big tides like this, the sea went out quickly for the first important distance and this was where his nets were set, at the edge of the high water mark, so he calculated they would be lying open three hours before the low tide.

Early in the year, sometimes he had risked leaving the nets down for two tides, leaving them in the midnight ebbs, and the fish that had lain in the net from the first tide would be clean inside, with their vents dug out where the minute crabs had gone into them and eaten the guts of them out. Birds generally went for the heads and he hadn't had a bird caught in the net ever and he was thankful for that because it was a small dread to him.

He could see the scallopers out on the five-mile line and he thought of the great difference between pulling a trigger and pulling a dredger, and of the personal deliberateness in one and the indiscrepancy of the other.

They opened up the beds, and the scallop boats on the horizon had arrived strangely one night as a line of lights almost like a village strung out along the furthest line of sight. At Christmas they were joined by further boats and the sea at night looked decorated. They had worked the beds for months, dredging with heavy nets loaded down with iron frames.

A month or so ago, a man went overboard and after searching for hours all the boats came in that day from respect, and Hold had some sense that something in that man must have wanted to have gone, because, Hold thought, it must be difficult to fall into the sea from a big boat.

He thought of the dredgers and he thought of their netted iron buckets smashing blindly over the seabed and how the men on the boats did not have to see the making of the desert they would bring about; and he thought: there are forces that work that way in everything that happens.

And perhaps in that moonlight he thought too much. And he thought whether it was better to make choices, and to take directions and risk a net being there; or whether it was best to stay bedded somewhere, and risk some great thing being dragged through you. And he thought how Danny had died, and how that was like some great thing dragged through him, and how it had left the bed he'd made smashed and damaged and disanchored. And how, for a very long time afterwards, the people who were close to him couldn't see where they were in the sand.

He collected the three rabbits he

had shot and laid them out side by side on the turf and put the bag onto the grass and went down on his haunches using the rifle for balance. He took out the gun bag and checked the rifle over once more and then put it away and lay the gun bag down.

It was important to paunch the rabbits immediately so the meat would not change, and one by one he took the rabbits and cleaned them, cutting the glistening ropes of gut and the stomachs out to lie on the ground as some bonanza of his surgery. It was an unusual thing to use the knife of his friend which was usually for fish but he had found a way with it, and he used it out of sentiment and a sense from somewhere that a man did not need more than one knife.

For a moment, there was moonlight, the inside of a shell, some shard caught in the dark mass of that eye, a part moon reflected as he held the rabbit down.

He knelt in the cropped turf and dry sea thrift and finished the last rabbit and, before cutting them, with his thumb he had peed the rabbits by forcing out the last urine from their bladder.

There was a constancy without rhythm to the sea below, swelling and crushing with almost a machine-like quality with that same sense it had contained within itself for days. Like some broken metronome for the earth. Just from the sound he knew how the breakers would look, moving up from the fluid sea as if great boastful shoulders were beneath them, then crushing down. It was like a wrestler throwing someone. It was as if Hold acknowledged those thuds somewhere inside him, like acknowledging a stronger man.

He could see the clouds scud slightly and lift in the sky and start to move, and knew they would come over in a little while and wondered if, after he'd worked the nets, it would be darker and easier to shoot on the cliffs afterwards. But there was something inside him this night that did not feel like shooting, and it was part of the same thing that had stopped him waking the boy.

He wiped the oily blood and fluids off his hands in the short dew covered grass and knelt on the bag for a while looking at the rabbits. The guts were warm, and steamed. He was suddenly and briefly tired. And in that moonlight he felt it would be nice to build a house around himself and sleep. He pushed from his mind the thought that it would have been nice to walk into that room and lie down with her and begin something. He hoped it would stay brotherly. He hoped they could keep it like that.

He got up and picked up the rabbits and had the emptiness for them that he had momentarily with the wild things he killed, because of the perfection they had and which tame things could never possess. The white in their fur showed up in the moon and they were the colour of fish for a moment, glistening silver. Then they seemed to dull, to become dark patches in his hands.

He put the rabbits in the bag and clipped it up and took out the head torch and shone it just from his hands and went on down towards the cliff path to the beach. Here and there on the coast that swept the bay, towns showed like the last glowing ashes of settling fireplaces. The rest of the coast was dark, permanent, impassive to the pleading sea which beat in with a steady, repeated argument against the wreck of the shore.

He could imagine, years ago, the sea, its temper lost in storm and the dark chaos of that bay. And he saw in his mind the huge fires lit on the headlands, the lost ship come to those false beacons and dashed in those waves against the coast, its goods torn out and strewn upon the shore. And he reflected how, for this to happen, there must have been whole villages treacherous for this collection, who were not pirates in their minds, but who were like fishermen or farmers in their industry. He thought of the boy and of what he had said and of the possibility that there was treasure on the beach from this great slaughter, and as he passed, in a field he saw a herd of curlew over the ground, and they were ghostly and strange in that light.

He cut down to the beach in that dark tunnel of torchlight, with the scree of rock ancient-formed, split and busted down the edge of the path. The iron rust showed in the rock and the smooth shale bedewed reflected and he felt for once that it was he the strange thing here. How the curlews had undone their compactness at him, and lost their peace as if he was not something fearful, but to them impossible.

He hopped down the foot or so drop from where the cliff fell away to the beach and the sense of the beach was immediate, like jumping into water. A change underfoot in the clack of the flat and uneven conglomerate beach stones where he stepped. He turned off the head torch and let his eyes adjust as if coming out of that tunnel of light. It was as if the types of light that night had been stored here, and were being harboured, or here and there given back by the lines of quartz in the fallen rock, and the flat wet stones. There was a strong smell of salt.

He walked up the beach, arcing out from the cliffside to where there was enough blue, predominant light to see by, and taxied his way over the uneven stones at the edge of the pools.

The sea had been up high leaving little of the beach clear and the tidemark was lost in the shadow of the cliffs where the moonlight didn't reach. The beach changed quickly and he turned on the head torch again and came off the rocks and up a bank of gravel and onto the long, feminine shapes of sea-smoothened fallen shale that stretched under the cliffs to the point.

Whenever he stood here, he felt some sense of affinity. The shapes were amazing in that strange light. It was an affinity of place and time. Some gentle sense that he was simply part of a process. Then he felt it, and it was very brief. That he was being watched.

He stopped and listened. Just the sea. The hollow boom of the rocks it moved as it broke and sucked at the beach. The trinkets of sound where water sheeted down the cliffs, running spare off the fields above. Nothing. Just the white sense of it.

There had been some change. A drop in temperature, an increase in the breeze, and his heightened senses had felt it. It was childlike. Some greater adrenaline in him. Some thing he could not stop when he went to the nets, an expectation that did not exist anywhere else in his life. He was unwatched. He was sure of that. Unwatched. That he was simply imagining.

81

In the moonlight you could make out the beach and have a sense of it, but when you switched on the torch there was just the tunnel of light, and everything outside it stopped existing. And while there was reassurance in this stretch of light, it was work not to think of those things that could suddenly be possible beyond it.

When his father was at home, he'd had to develop a way to survive the otherwise destructive atmosphere he brought and it had become like a mechanism in him, this ability to force out thought. It was what allowed him to do what he did, and helped him not to tear himself up. Sometimes this worked against him, but it helped him to exist his way. He knew that you just had to push out indecision and distractions in the way you had to not be scared of the dark. He was very determined in this and, in the light of the choices he made, everything around these choices disappeared.

He went on over the big rocks, the cragged and damaged boulders where the beach turned round to make a little false bay, and he saw the white floats of the net laid out across the pools.

He could see the turned and roping line where the net was and that there was a fish in it, against the black stone a broad scimitar silver in that moonlight. An earring of metal. He thrilled to see it early.

He kept beneath the cliff and would not look again from some self-invented ritual and got to the end of the net and took off the gun and the game bag. Then he walked up the net picking round the dark heaps of wrack and the light-emitting pools. There were three fish low in the net. A big mullet and two bass, and higher up the net the bass he had seen immediately. At the moment the bass would not be in shoals and it was more usual to catch this many fish, not the vast catch of them you could get later on. He knew from gutting them that they were coming in for the early peeler crab, hunting the soft-shells of their growing bodies.

At the top of the net was a spider crab, insectile, like some long, mechanical thing that had flown into a web. Just beyond the net the rocks were cemented with sand that looked like a grater with the riddles of sandworms. The sea breaking on it made a sound like the airbrakes of a big lorry. The sound was more of a smash out by the spit of rocks which broke sublittoral out of the sea some hundred yards away and that you could see now and were uncovered in this massive tide.

He felt this sense again, of being watched. It was unlike him. He looked down at the spider crab. He had no sympathy with them in the way he did with other things. The other crabs had been in the pots that were some way out and this was the first really close in this year, and was early and it was unnerving in its earliness, but there would be more. A swarm, so much more efficient than our native crabs, that comes inshore from the deeper water as the water warms. They were aliens. Something sent. They seemed built for some other purpose and to exist in some mass. He could see the gulls and kittiwakes white against the cliffs and was sure, by some sense, that something passed on the sea, some cloud of shearwaters nocturnal.

He chilled, and chided himself. There was some portentous thing on the beach that night, and he had to say to himself: if I am watched it is by fox or bird, not man, and there is nothing but fox or bird or man or things of their material, there can be nothing else. Just then a breaker thudded. A seventh wave perhaps. And it was a very big sound. The pullback had a brag to it. Like it was poking fun it felt.

He headed back to the bottom of the net, picking his way with the torchlight over the awkward pools that stretched the thirty metres back. There were weird patches of dark and light in the sky where the moon came or not through the shifting cloud now and, with the torch on, the beach looked very dark. It gave it even more of a sense of enclosure with the white sound of the sea. Like there was a presence very close around you.

Hold put the bands of the torch around his head and crouched down to the net and started to work the fish out, undoing the problem in his head, working the looped nylon over the fins, away from the hard lids of the gills, out from the articulate bones of the mouth. You had to try to see how the fish had hit. Whether it had writhed and spun or tried to go on. Then you took it out, freeing the net, as if you were swimming it backwards. He worked with that flat deliberate patience you have to have and, in that cave of light he made for himself, there was just this in his mind and it was a great easing to do just the one thing.

The mullet came free and he held it by the great bony head so its thick lips seemed to pout at him and he lay it down and in the torchlight its loosened scales reflected back off his hands. It was a big heavy fish and the scales were bigger than thumbnails and he knew that the meat would be very good. They were difficult to sell because of the flavour of soil and the disturbing muddiness of flesh that mullet had when you caught them in estuaries or harbours, where they filtered sewage and pastes for food. But when you caught them on the rocks like this the flesh was firm and white and strong and froze well enough.

He went on to the bass. There was a ferocity to it even lying there, some angular, predatory quality. Blood rimed the gills and the torn fins where it had refused to stop fighting the net, recusant of the fact that once it had turned into it, it was caught and there was no fight it could make. There seemed still fury in its eye that would not forgive itself, as if it scoured itself for some signal it had missed that would have shown the net was there. Yet, there has to be decision. A way must be taken. He thought for a moment that the fish might still be alive. In the torchlight he kept coming back to that eye, so different it was from the droll, herbivorous eye of the mullet. Hunter or gatherer, both had turned themselves into the net. The mullet had looked more at peace with itself though, as if it believed though saddened and ended that it had made the choice in the best of faiths. As he undid the bass from some last traps of nylon, Hold knew that these thoughts were a ridiculous romanticism, and that there could be no peace in dying in this way. He had killed them, that was his responsibility.

There was a scrape of stones beyond his sight and he looked up to the cliffs and saw nothing, simply the impassivity responding. Again the sound came and the loose shale flashed in his headlight and he looked up the scree to see a rabbit bump away to some safer bank. Then he saw it, as he turned his head back out to sea. Something on the water. He ripped off the torch and hid its light against him and crouched and had no idea why this was his reaction. He turned the torch off, holding the net as if it was some safe thing.

As his eyes altered to the dark, the small landscape grew back round him, coming in patches as his eyes focused. The humps of wrack. The pools. The grated sand. Dawn had brought a preminiscent light to the horizon which hid the scallop lights and which somehow made the sea look darker. There was light from the moon, some thin aureole, misting into the shifted clouds. He heard the rubber hit the rock, the strange, stretching sound like a creaking floor and he felt himself fizz with electricity. It could be someone come to poach the nets. He thought often about things coming to that, about that challenge coming like a violent dog. Don't back down. And he turned on the light and stood up.

His face was set. He was ready to respond, or to call out, and he put all the look he could into his shoulders and his arms, and the pump of the breaker came loudly and he set his feet and then the sound again came, an unmistakable impact, over the rising beat of his heart. He thought of the gun back on the stones above the pools.

The inflatable was spinning slowly by the rocks. The army grey of it full and neutral at the edge of the torch beam. It looked unmanned, but it was in the end of the beam, as if it consumed the light. Like something circling the edge of a clearing. He saw a flash of engine, some red perhaps as the boat swung. And then a heap. A dark mass in the belly of the boat and he knew immediately it was a man.

He could feel the adrenaline surge through him and his mind turned to one repeated curse word but there was something in that very clear. He put on the head torch and went out, footing over the rocks to the easier sand and then he went into the sea, stumbling under the power of the breakers for safe space for his feet.

87

There was real strength in the water and the waves were high and big and it took a few seconds for the cold water to get through his clothes and the extreme cold was like a shock that his adrenaline fought.

He waded at the boat through the tunnel of light he made, having to fight the push and draw of the water, the cold sting and salt reaching his thighs as he went out. He hardly had any thought, it was just an automatic thing to do.

The boat was a few metres away and moving out and he was slow, putting his feet down blindly through the dragging water, and the swell was much bigger by the rocks. The water smashed him, one big wave that nearly took him over, and he found a handhold half submerged against the rock and held on and then he went out with the draw of the tide half floating at the boat which was very close now. It came at him with a thump and hit him hard and he held to it with the wind hit half out of him and went backwards with it, his legs sucked underneath its hull. Then the sea sighed again as if setting itself and he scrambled for a footing and dug his fingers into the cord around the gunwale and tried to go with the boat in the new onrush of water. He reached the rock and clung hard against the dragging ebb and the boat stayed with him this time. He was up to his stomach in water on some unseen risen stone or slope of grit and it was like the boat would come no further with the draw of that outward tide too strong a force of gravity for him to beat.

His breath came spitting through his teeth and his eyes stung and it was all he could do to hold the boat there with the cold starting to wear through the thin, fleeting first retch of adrenaline. He tried to swallow in strength from the air and the torch moved as his head did, up into the air for breath in a disorientating way. I have to still, he thought. Still. Just still a minute. He held the boat going up and lowering on the swell with all his muscles stubborn and hoping that he could get more from himself. He held it for a while until he could get some clarity, as if the energy would go out of the boat like holding down a brawling man. He tried to keep his head steady.

Behind him the waves were busting on the reef of sand and tearing out past him and driving shards of gravel into him. Salt stung in a graze he hadn't noticed. And then the boat seemed to make its own decision and wrenched round and lodged itself on a point of rock, and it too seemed to still, as if it needed breath.

The body was by his face now. 'Christ,' Hold was thinking. 'I guess here it is.' He could see the man heaped in the boat. The man wore all black, or so it looked in that light, with a big puffer jacket that gave him a comfortable, sleeping look. He shook him. He thought again about the rifle on the shore. He leaned as far as he could and punched the leg. Hold grabbed the collar and pulled the man and sat him up and the head came up and sat itself up as if against a pillow and it was like the broken neck of a bird. He had the high cheekbones and wide face of a Slav.

The boat seemed to be suspended in that patch of water, and the two men were going up and down with the swell. Hold called at the man and then pulled his ear and just stood there holding the boat knowing the man was dead. He just tried to hold on, with the stinging water hitting him, and it was like his ability to make a decision was in the same suspended place as the boat.

What the hell had happened here? A scalloper? He knew that there were crew from all over, perhaps going between ships for something. The boat was bare and without markings. Had he run out of fuel? Hold stretched to the motor pump and squeezed the bulb and felt some resistance that meant there was a little fuel at least, and then saw the can and tried to reach it with an outstretched finger. It was full.

In the torchlight the face looked very white and flat. I have to get him ashore, thought Hold. I have to find something more from myself and get him ashore.

He felt this sudden massive emptying tiredness as if this one thing was finally too much. Then it rang. He saw the glow first, a white shade. He half leapt at the man to reach him, draw him closer and went for the pocket and the phone fell into the boat, flashing soundlessly, then there were three pitching beeps and the battery went. 'Shit,' said Hold, out loud. And then it all came to him, in the first relief of this first utterance and he swore and swore out loud and hit the side of the boat in this futile thing.

In his anger, the boat was starting to go out again and he couldn't hold it, but the anger itself came into him like this extra fuel. *I have to think quickly now. Think. Come on. It's happened now, you're in it. Do something, even if you can't hold the boat.*

He braced himself against the rock and held the cord and unzipped the man's jacket and felt inside for wallet or card, the water starting to beat him again, for some sign of his name. And then he felt the water get a purchase and pull him off the rock and in his new found anger he got a strength in him and felt all the sick, balling fear in him alight and he yanked the boat and went into the water holding it, and up to his chest he spat his defiance at the sea as it came in through his gritted teeth and finding the ground under his feet he dragged the boat like some furious and stubborn horse and went towards the dark beach with everything he had, cursing and screaming.

When he got the boat nearly to the reef of sand it came finally with him in an angry run, knocking him to the stones as it beached itself. It had taken on water. On the beach the cold hit Hold. He tried to get his head round that and just held it like some solid fact to deal with later. You have to get up, he said. Don't get cold. You have to get up.

He shut the man's eyes and picked up the phone and tried to switch it on but it just flashed briefly, bleeped and went out. Then he collapsed on the reef of sand.

The torch was dimming and going out. He switched it off for a while and just sat there looking at the shape of the boat and the dead man in the moonlight.

He got up and tried to walk a little

of the stiff coldness out and went back to the boat. The grit and broken shells and sand that had been washed into his shoes grazed him, but it was pointless to try and do anything about that now. He knew he was hurt. It's amazing what you can't feel in the sea. The lume of the dawn was building and the bay was filled with this strange ancient light and he could hear turning in the energy of the tide.

He checked the man over again, went through the pockets, and lifted him to see if there were any other parts to his fairy tale in the boat, and then he took another look at the Slavic face. The wind was starting to lick up with the tide change and he bit with cold and was suddenly very hungry. He thought for a moment about taking the man's jacket that was drier than his. Somehow in his coldness and hunger was a sense of his own reality. He clung on to that.

Gulls were coming off the cliffs and circling and began to call and other birds were beckoning in the new light. He was shaking his hands to get them warm. What if someone was here to meet him, Hold thought. Suddenly it was to him as if the light was some enemy, some thing that would see him. He thought back to the stones falling on the cliff earlier. I cannot have been seen, he said. There was no one. Then he saw the packages.

There were three of them, carefully wrapped, bound up in parcel tape, all about the size of a fist. He picked them up. Some thing inside him knew already they were packages of some dangerous, exploiting thing which he felt a sick fear of in his gut. It was like they could speak.

He dragged the boat a little further onto the reef and went back to the game bag and took out the knife. Then he cut a thin split in one of the parcels with the knowledge of what was in them already in him. A small, sticky spill of white powder sat up out of the split. It smelt strange on the knife. He had no idea what it was. But he knew it was drugs, and it looked raw and unprocessed and he wouldn't be able to tell you what part of his knowledge told him this.

He looked at the parcel in his hand and thought of the worth of it and of the house and of Danny and the dead Slav and of a risk that would surely only have been taken for great wealth.

'Now what?' he said. And then he sat on the rock with the parcels in his hand, the light coming.

He'd had this image of Cara with her neck in a net, tiring herself to a beaten point of exhaustion. Of his mother. Take it, he had thought. Take this now, and try to change things, or you will have to stand by and watch it all again.

'I couldn't have been seen,' he thought. 'No one could have seen this.'

Part Two

He could not take everything. He had
not intended to bring the net in and had no bag for it.
There were the big fish and the rabbits. The rifle had
to come. He was like a point of concentration now,
with the mechanism from childhood fully kicked in.

As soon as he saw them, he knew he would take
the packages. He had thought briefly about taking the
boat, of checking the engine for serial numbers, of
weighting the man and throwing him in the water and
had known this was madness. He knew he must have
no connection with the packages, and he must
disappear off the beach.

He went back to the net and started to take the
other fish out with his numb hands, trying to slow
himself in this process, and the light was growing bit
by bit, even giving some luminosity to the strands of
nylon as if it was becoming animate. He got the knife

and cut out the fish and dumped it on the rocks and cut out the other fish and there was something almost religious about cutting the net, like he had broken some sanctity and that he had cut much more than the net in doing this thing. He went to the tangled crab and cut it free and cut and pulled away the threads amongst it and put it down on the rock so as not to hurt even this thing he had no like of. And he moved efficiently in this place of decision he had built for himself and pulled up the anchoring rope of the net from the bowl of rocks he had it in, ignoring the criminality of having cut the net.

He threw the fish down the beach and got the large plastic sack he carried for them and arm over arm piled the yards of net into it, tearing automatically at the large arms of seaweed that were amongst it. He thought about putting the net in the boat and of keeping the fish but he knew that should not be done; and he thought too about taking the fish and leaving the net lifted, and of bringing round the fishing boat and sculling out to collect it so much was his reluctance to leave the fish and to kill for no purpose. At least the gulls will have them, he thought. The bay was filling with light now and it was the point of most coldness.

He worked his hands trying to warm them and sucked at his fingers to bring the blood back to them and tasted the fish and salt water on them and the iodine tang of the weed. He put on the torch and took the rabbits from the bag and the nylon line and blunt needle for stitching the net and he cut out the liver and kidneys and hearts he had left in the rabbits and threw them too on the beach and washed his hands in a pool and watched the dark strings of blood come off him. As cold as he was, the water felt warm on his hands.

He took the packages one by one and set them inside the rabbits and one by one stitched up the cavities, forcing the needle though the taut hide with a pebble and the rabbits grew in weight and seemed to reconstitute their missing shape like they underwent some backward act of resurrection.

He had sat wondering what to do and everything had happened unconsciously, as if the decisions were being made at some distance from him, and he had none of the usual discussion in his mind about what choices to make. It was as if he already knew. He had sat and stared at the boat and at the heap of man and down at his fish and had taken out the fish scales and weighed the packages one by one, hanging them by their loops of tape. And he knew that for a man to take a boat, to take this weight of things somewhere, there had to be much value in those things and he had sat for a while with his head in his hands.

He looked once more at his scattered bounty of fish and took his knife and went to the boat and took the spare fuel and re-filled the tank and pumped the fuel through to the motor. Then he dragged the man into the back of the boat. He took the bow of the boat by the cord and heaved it round until it met the water and walked in with it, feeling the cold water come into him again and the man bounce in the bed of the boat and he let it ride over the waves and went with it into the deeper water.

He dropped the motor and pulled out the weed that had dragged in the propeller and took the gunwale cord and cut it with the knife, going backwards with the boat each time a wave came to it. Then he wrapped the cord over and over round the prop shaft and fed an end of it through the rings as if it might have snapped and gone itself around the engine. And as strongly as he could in the water he stayed the motor so it could not turn and pushed the boat back out into the deeper water.

He checked the prime on the motor once more and moved the choke and pressed the automatic starter and swore silently at the motor when it did not start. And then he cut off the toggle and took out the drawstring from the man's hood and unscrewed the cap of the flywheel as the boat kept going back at the beach and he kept walking it forward. He had cut his hand somehow and it was bleeding heavily onto the wheel and he wrapped the drawstring round the wheel and tugged and sent it round and the engine spat and fired and he levelled the choke and felt the blood go down his hand. And then he dropped a gear and coughed at the spume of fuel that caught him and he let the boat go.

It cut out through the water over the waves like some thing released and he watched it until it was way out in its straight line. Then he got out of the water, took his things, and watched until he couldn't see the boat any more. Then he walked laden off the beach.

He dropped the net by the van.

He was shaking with exhaustion and cold and nervous and he could hardly move. His arms were numb with the effort of carrying the wet net.

He got the net in the back of the van and took out an old sack and spread it automatically on the driver's seat. The places his body hurt were becoming known to him one by one as the anaesthetic effects of the adrenaline and the shock settled into a low sick-tasting weight in his stomach.

'Don't do this,' he thought. 'Take it to the police and turn it all in now.'

It was light now, and the blackbirds and thrushes were vibrant with sound. He sat there for a while. He thought of Danny and his belief in the outside chance.

'No,' he thought. 'It's fallen to you. You kind of asked for something like this. You have to take it on now.'

*

He drove back to the caravan and took the rabbits in and put them on the unit in the bag. He took out the phone from the pocket in the bag and dried it and put it from some inexplicable paranoia inside the grill section of the cooker. Then he took out the rabbits from the bag and looked at them and then he took them out and hung them in the van back thinking that would be natural, and that the van was most difficult to get into. I cannot be too careful now, he thought. There is no part of me which can miss something.

He was sure he was not seen but he understood what he had done and what he had started and how he had come into something very dangerous. He looked around the caravan. He locked the door and then he took the ball of string he'd hung the rabbits up with and he ran a line from the handle of the door to the open bathroom door and pushed the bathroom door back until the line was tight and then he wedged the bathroom door. He took the rifle from the case and checked it and laid it down on the unit by the bathroom door with its chamber open and he left the silencer off. *I cannot at any point let myself think that I am being too paranoid*. The extra sound of the unsilenced gun might give me split seconds if it happened. He looked around again and checked the line to see that it was tight enough to pull the bathroom door if the front door opened. He put a handful of cartridges on the shelf by the bathroom door, took the rifle, and went into the shower.

This involves only me, he had thought. This will only affect me, and if I do it right it will solve everything. He had sat on the rock, not really feeling the cold as if it was a thing far distant from himself, as if he had become his own voice of fate.

He knew. He simply knew he would take the parcels and that the boat had been delivered up to him and all that was left was to articulate this knowing in himself. Things come along and the rest of everything depends on what we can do with the things that come along, and we shouldn't make decisions out of fear.

He thought of the pointless death of the man and of the boat being delivered up to him on the beach and thought vaguely that the death would take on purpose if it was to secure things for Cara and Jake.

He knew what he should do. Secure the boat and call the police. But for what, then? Even as he had these arguments with himself he went through the things he needed to do and the way he would do them. The old mechanisms of surviving his father were already kicking in.

He looked down at the packages. He thought wildly about buying a boat, but first of the responsibility towards Cara and Jake. *Think of the solution this represents to them*, he thought. It was one big answer, if he could see it through. It involves only me. There is a limit to how wrong it can go.

*

101

He had to find strength to take his clothes off. They peeled off in drunk layers leaving his body stinging with the air on it.

Naked, he sat and rubbed off the sand and grit that had stuck in the congealing grazes at his ankles where the tops of his shoes had been. His feet had swollen with the water and were raw and angry and blistered.

He washed off the dried blood from his hand in the sink and looked at the precise, deep scoring cut. He felt a deadweight in his arms, like a bruising, and knew this was just tiredness. He could see on his hip the love bite marks of the rock where he had smashed into it holding the boat and could feel the same dull, burning throb of pain in the shoulder that would come out as bruising in a few days; and then he stepped into the shower and just let all of those places hurt and sting as his body slowly came back to him.

He stayed in the shower until the tank ran out and then he took his towel and dried himself and went through to the bed and, exhausted, lay down.

When he woke up he was violently sick. He was woken by the screeching of magpies and the panicking clicking of the small birds as they raided their new nests. He had slept for barely an hour, and the sleep was something he could do nothing about.

When he had finished being sick he washed out his mouth and stood up. That was the last of it. That's it gone now, he told himself. The bullets and the gun were still in the bathroom and he put them away methodically.

He took some painkillers and ate some plain ham from the fridge and made a coffee and sat down. The caravan was like a goldfish bowl. 'Everywhere's going to feel that way for a while,' he thought.

He finished the coffee and got some money and put the rifle in the van and drove out. He went to the garage and bought a coolbag and some antiseptic cream and a multiple phone charger and filled up the van and asked to use the telephone directory. He said he had to find some numbers for a driving instructor for a friend and he pretended to find that and on his way wrote down the number that he wanted.

He drove out of the town to a phone box that he knew and he called the number.

When he came out of the call box he sat in the car for a while and just looked out down the road and watched the clouds bunch up over the mountains inland. 'Well, I'm in it now,' he said. Then he started the van up and took the back roads home.

Grzegorz stood in the office.

'What have you got to say for yourself?'

His line manager, another Pole, translated, even though Grzegorz got the drift. His line manager acted like some kind of self-appointed union man. He had it in for Grzegorz. Grzegorz had no idea why.

'It was being thrown out,' said Grzegorz. The line manager translated. 'It was going into the bins, I didn't steal it.'

'Don't we pay you enough?'

Actually, the pay was pretty good. It was as much as he could expect without any formal skills. 'I didn't steal. I wouldn't steal,' said Grzegorz.

He was careful to look remorseful but underneath was this bitter anger. He wanted to throw things back in the man's face. He saw his job disappearing, felt this humiliating fury that they had this power over him. That they could dangle him on a string. They could change his life, just like that.

'We're quite clear on such things. It's a criminal offence.'

The line manager didn't translate, but talked back to the man. He was donning this friendship with Grzegorz and it made him sick. 'Now I'll owe him,' he thought. 'He thinks he's fatherly. He'll push me round all the more.' He felt he wanted to smash the two men's faces together. Grzegorz listened with this blurred concentration as the two men talked about him, juggled with his life as if it was a toy. 'They always have to keep you in line,' he thought to himself, angrily.

'It's okay, we've had a talk,' said the line manager to Grzegorz in Polish.

'We could dismiss you for this,' said the man. Grzegorz ignored him.

'He's dropping you to minimum shifts.'

He'd been working all the hours he could, trying to build up a nest egg. They were laying people off at his wife's factory as well.

'They just want to keep you down,' he thought.

'Minimum shifts,' said the man. 'There's plenty of men want the work.'

Grzegorz had a vision of strangling the man with the tripe. He was sure he could smell it on his clothes now. That was the smell of poorness. It was in everything. You couldn't get it out.

The remnants of snowdrops were still

up and, in the woods just at the end of the farm lane, the late crocuses were through and the pigeon pecked at the little flags of petal, ruining them.

The woodpigeon cooed briefly and found a stick from the ivy and the leaves on the ground and lifted it with his beak and measured its weight, getting the stick balanced like a trapeze artist would. He could hear the van some way off and it was part of the world's noises to him. He dropped the stick and went back to ruining the crocuses. He could hear the van come closer down the thin road, and hear its engine change tone with the gear changes.

The road was flanked on one side by blackthorn, and on the other by the steep bank that was the edge of a woodland and that would be all bluebells come May. On the bank were strangles of holly and the oak and beech leaves had fallen and the snowdrops were secretly amongst them.

The other side, beyond the blackthorn hedge, there were a few slim and damp-looking fields that made a skirt against the river, flanked mostly by oak and hazel that had grown thin and twisted up and unmanaged so close to the water.

The small river rose in the hills and began its way as a thin white stream that very quickly clattered over rocks before spreading out into a shallow bed and meandering into the small and severe valley that was the cwm.

By the time it reached the valley floor, the river was less urgent and slid gently past the road to the sea. It was this river which came out near the beach where Hold fished, and because the salmon and sewin ran that river, he had to keep the nets a certain way from its mouth.

Hold took the van over the little hump of the stone bridge and glimpsed the river as he went over and saw the syrupy look of it, and here and there the white, bursting energy.

The pigeon flicked up off the floor to a nearby

tree, puffing his deep breast. He scanned the pale grey road. The grey of the asphalt was a very dead grey compared to him.

The van got closer. You could hear the gears shifting down in sound at the wide corner a small way off. The pigeon looked back at the crocuses on the end of the farm lane that had been planted there deliberately along with tiny narcissi. The little narcissi were almost open and you could sense the energy from underground in them.

The pigeon cooed and the white van appeared on the corner and the pigeon could see the roadside reflected off the sheen of the windscreen and the man driving. At this strange thing, the pigeon took off in a clatter of sticks.

Hold shifted gears, changed down again as the van complained and chided himself for not having his mind on the driving, and for a split second, in that change of gear, there was a stall in momentum. No motion.

The pigeon crashed out from the trees in front of the van and, suddenly panicked by the open space before him to the river, tried to cut back into the cover of the woods. He was instantly aware of the mistake in that split second decision and the sparrowhawk hit him.

The sparrowhawk had driven the pigeon into the open space and hit him with the concentrated impact of an ambush.

The pigeon had a quick vision of the sparrowhawk

107

then the thing hit him, and he felt his light bones smash under the force, and his proud chest burst, and his neck broke in the whiplash of the hit.

The bird seemed to burst in front of Hold and the pigeon went sideways like a ball hit from a bat. He flicked the brake and went under the feathers which seemed to hang in the air and in the corner of his eye he saw the pigeon crash off the crown of blackthorn and go over into the field.

In the mirror he could just see the feathers come down and behind them the strewn crocuses on the farm lane, and he held the van steady on the road.

'One wrong move,' he thought. 'That's all it takes. One wrong move.'

The phone call had been to an anonymous drugs advice service and the rigmarole of acting as if he thought his son was selling drugs led up to that one question:

'How much per kilo, if it is cocaine?'

It had sounded like it was cocaine. The white, pearly powder.

'Forty to fifty thousand.'

He was on the beach digging cockles.

There were about forty of them and they'd picked them up with a bus and driven them down to the beach. The sea looked very distant but they were warned of the speed the tide would come in. 'It's faster than a horse,' they said. Then they unloaded the rakes and buckets and walked out onto the long, flat sand.

He could handle this. This was outdoor work. It was backbreaking, working quickly in the gap of the tide, but against the ache he could always look up from the rucked wet sand to the sea far out, catching the light with this sense of massive space. It was like the flat fields of home, just this endless, empty plain. It was nice to be amongst things that did not belong to man.

He raked up the top few inches of sand, hearing the shells of the cockles click ceramically on the tines of the rake, then he gathered them into the bucket. He could do this work well, but it was sporadic and not reliable. It was a good extra, but that was it. It was off the books, undeclared income and he knew there was a risk if he was caught that they would send him back. But he needed the money. And by now, he had grown a defiant little seed against things.

He stopped for a drink and watched the gulls off on the sandbank away from them. There was the sound all round him of the work, the workers dotted about the beach, and there was the feeling of practical calmness that is in very old types of work.

'I could do this. I could do this thing,' he thought.

The man came up and took Grzegorz's bucket and put down an empty. He checked the weight of the bucket.

'You do this work well,' said the man. It was all in Polish.

'It's just like soil,' Grzegorz said.

The man hefted the bucket again and assessed Grzegorz.

'What's your name?' he asked. Grzegorz told him, and he told him where he was from out of the now automatic habit of saying it.

'You're a farmer, Grzegorz Przybylski,' said the man.

'I was,' Grzegorz said.

'And now?'

'Slaughterhouse,' Grzegorz said. He could feel his body cementing up from the uneasy half-bent position of the raking and wanted to get on with the work before he got cold. They were paid by their weights, he didn't have time to talk.

The man nodded. 'Family?'

'Yes,' said Grzegorz. 'I have a wife, two boys.' He was suspicious of the man, knowing the danger of the undeclared work.

'And where are you living?'

'In one of the agency houses.' He bent to work again.

'Still?' said the man. 'How many?'

'There's twenty-eight of us there,' Grzegorz said.

The man nodded. Then he looked over Grzegorz and walked away.

'This could be the thing,' thought Grzegorz. 'You

wouldn't need much. You'd just need a rake, a bucket, some transport and someone to buy the shells off you. A man on his own probably couldn't do much, but if there was a group of us. Four or five people, two carloads maybe.' He'd heard of the cockle beds further north. They were public land. He'd heard that up there, they reckoned there was half a million pounds worth of cockles in the bay at any one time. 'Half a million pounds. Even Ana could work. We could be together. She could go back and forth with the buckets. The kids when they are old enough, when they're not in school. How much would it cost, really?' he thought. 'To set that up. Not much.'

'Did the man talk to you?' Harry said on the bus.

'No,' said Grzegorz. 'Which man?'

'The bucket man.'

'Maybe I had a different bucket man from you,' he said.

'Well, he asked if I knew you.'

'What did he want?' The bus smelled of the muddy saltness. There was a group of Asians in the back and they made a strange, alien noise in their talk.

'He said he was going to talk to you. He said if he didn't get a chance I should talk to you.'

Grzegorz could feel the tiredness from the work growing in him. He was trying to hold on to the sense of the long space of the beach. He thought of the idea

111

of his own business, the little money he'd need for that.

'They're looking for some men to do a job.'

He plugged in the mobile and switched on the socket and put it down on the unit and saw the bars appear on it, pulsing like something medical as if it registered his pulse. He switched it on.

He scanned awkwardly through the missed calls and dialled numbers and the message alert flashed and vibrated. The text said the voicemail box was filled with voicemails. He pressed okay but that didn't take him to them.

He flicked through until he found the text messages and tried to read them. Most of the messages were signed with an A. They were not in English. He found the sent messages box and read the foreign words meaninglessly in the one sent message. He felt nervous and wrong with the phone.

He looked through at the times of the calls and saw they were from all times of day and that they stopped three days ago. He flicked through to the photographs. He guessed the woman was A.

There were a few shots of her. Her face was plain and strong and looked like it had been through things. In some of the shots she had a baby and there was another young child, and there was one shot of the child sitting with the baby like he'd been made to sit there for the photograph. He had the high broad cheekbones of the man in the boat.

Hold took off the back of the phone and undid the battery and looked at the SIM card for the provider and then he used his own mobile to call for the number of a phone shop. 'Anywhere,' he said. 'Okay. Manchester.'

He wrote down the number and called the shop and said that he'd bought a new phone and forgotten his voicemail number and they told him the number to dial from the handset to get the messages.

He put the other phone back together and switched it back on and had to go through some procedure to reset the language and time and date because he'd taken off the battery.

He dialled the number the phone shop had given him and listened to the voice telling him how many messages he had and went through them one by one. A few of the messages were just silence, for just a few seconds. The others all were foreign. The first one or two messages sounded light, happy, and the kid came on for one of them and he could make out that he said 'tato' and instinctively knew it was like saying 'daddy'. Then he listened as the woman broke down. He listened as with each message the woman broke up into smaller and smaller pieces into the useless, unanswered phone.

When he sat down, he felt he had killed the man.

He switched the phone off. His head had started

swimming with the harrowing grief of the woman, and he had had to go cold, like when he had to kill things. One phrase, that she said over and over, had stuck itself into his mind, and it was difficult to forget and like seeing the eye of an animal you are about to kill look right in you. He couldn't make it out. *Vrooj prosser checkham*. She said it over and over. And *gzie yesters*. He wondered if *checkham* was the man's name. He couldn't shake the sound of it. In some ways that helped. It was helping him go cold, giving him that solid thing to react to.

He turned the phone back on. He had the speech in his head. Make the call, wait. He was sure he would know when he'd dialled the right number from the list and it took him a moment to register that taking out the battery had cleared the call history and he had no way of getting it back.

He'd tried the voicemails again and

tried calling the sender but the numbers in the blank messages – the people he needed to talk with – didn't allow it. He sat there looking at the phone. He knew it would ring eventually.

After a few hours it did and he stood there for what seemed like a very long time looking at it ring and not answering. He recognised her number from the text messages.

114

He picked it up and pressed the button and the sound of her crashing relief in that language almost threw him and he said 'English, English,' very slowly.

Her words were desperate and broken.

'He's dead.'

And there was just this collapsed sound. 'He's dead.' And she was quiet for a while.

'What's your address?' he said. 'Your address?'

And the strange language came again, harrowed, pleading over him in a wave, and he said, 'I want to send you some money,' and then there were sounds that were not words and were like the grating of a tide going out and he put down the phone.

He kept waiting. He realised that if the phone didn't ring he had no idea what to do with the packages. He thought of throwing them somewhere, of taking them and the phone on the boat and dumping them but he knew he couldn't. Some definite thing had taken him. He was prepared for moments of fear. He had to hold on to one belief. He kept thinking of the answer it would be, and of how it would change everything.

At one stage he texted her number with the message: Send your address and I can send you money. I am sorry about him. He realised he should never have sent it. Hearing that desperation he went in another notch, and felt how deeply he was in this thing.

He let two calls come through on his own phone

without answering and picked up the voicemails. The man was worried that he hadn't taken out the boat, and Cara called to say the man had called her. She was worried he was all right after knowing he was out last night. He phoned them both back and told them that he'd caught a chill.

Again, immediately, he knew it was a mistake. He didn't get chills. He didn't even use the word. He was making little mistakes. Simple mistakes. He should have called the man about the boat this morning. He should have called on Cara after the garage. Acted normally. He thought about the pigeon, about the falling feathers.

He forced himself to think. No more tiny mistakes. I have to think of everything.

For a while he sat there convinced they were stalling, giving themselves time to home in to the phone with some locator. That he would know nothing about it, they would track him. But he told himself that this was another phase of fear. He made himself eat. You have to be prepared for fear, he said. And you have to ride it out. He grilled the fillets he had caught yesterday and drank water and took more painkillers. The pain he could deal with but he wanted to keep the swelling down in case he had to move quickly. He was trying to think of everything. He was trying to be as methodical as he was with the gun.

116

When they called it was nearly dark.

'Where have you been?'

Hold waited, he felt okay. He could feel this mechanism in him.

'I have the package,' he said.

The voice said nothing for a moment, seemed to hover like somebody assessing a flavour.

'If you're using his phone you're an idiot. We already know where you are.'

Hold's brain was fireworking. He had the minute sense of being in a fight. Stick to one thing, he was saying to himself. Stick to one thing.

'There's no problem,' he said. 'I have the package.'

The voice seemed to pause again, breathe in.

'Where are you?' The tone was different. Beckoning.

'I'll bring you the package.'

The voice gave him instructions. He picked up in some of the voice that it was Liverpudlian.

'I'm closer to the other port,' Hold said.

'You'll get where you're told.'

Hold waited. He felt okay but the phone was slippery in his hand.

'By the way, you were seen.'

'Nobody saw me.' Hold pulled himself up. Stick to one thing. Stay on the one thing. No one had seen you. They don't know where you are. Stick to one thing.

'Is that a risk you want to take?' said the man.

'He's dead. I'll bring you the package. Where you said.'

The voice seemed to wait for a very long while.

'You know we know where his family is.' There was a veiled threat in that. 'If this is a set up.'

Hold repeated his instructions. Then said, 'It's not a set up.'

The voice waited again. Like it was looking through the phone. Tasting the air at the other end. Waiting.

Then Hold said it: 'The money?'

There was just business.

'You'll get the money.'

The phone rang off.

Part Three

The Scouser put the phone down

and sat back in the chair.

'Who are we going to use?' said the big redheaded man. The redhead had that kind of blond red hair and a firm, round face but his nose was messed all over it. It looked like it had never had a bone in it. He had strange, dog-like eyes almost.

The man in the chair considered and looked down at the phone as if it was a strange thing. He felt little needles of paranoia. He held everything before him, mentally, as if he was holding everything out in front of him in his hands. As if he could see everything. Was somebody inside engineering this? This was the second time parcels had gone missing recently.

He looked out of the window at the gaps in the houses and thought of bombs falling off target, this thing from a great height misguided and shattering into the buildings. What power, he thought. It would have been a better time to live in, a clearer time. You wouldn't have to brew this fear all the time, he thought. You wouldn't have to keep establishing it.

He felt the needles. Fear is necessary. Fear is an instrument. Fear makes people so much tamer. You just have to strike with great weight at the things people can't stop themselves caring for.

'Use the Irish,' he said. 'Let's keep this to ourselves.'

The weight of the packages that Hold had found was about a kilo. That was a street value of forty thousand pounds and the equivalent, when cut, of a thousand odd hits, maybe more.

The prime grade cocaine had come out of Colombia. The Poles were to be paid to carry a kilo into the mainland and hand it to a mule, who would move it on to the city.

Three-quarters of the world's annual yield of the drug is produced in Colombia. Its base product is the leaf of the coca tree, an innocuous looking plant farmed legally in Colombia. With its starry, five-petalled white flowers, you could mistake it for a blackthorn.

If they could afford them, the Indians who harvested the leaves flayed them up with petrol weed trimmers, or else simply poured them dried and pungent-smelling onto a thick tarpaulin that formed a pit of water. Then their families stamped the leaves down into a spinachy mash.

They added bags of chlorine and kerosene and sulphuric acid and stirred the mix with long wooden baffles and now and then the farmers would taste the kerosene. When they were ready, they skimmed off the kerosene which by taste they knew had drawn out the alkaloid and the rest of the mix they poured away onto the forest floor, the bleach and acid, to find its way into the river systems.

They strained the liquid through a cloth, then warmed the residue until it left a pasty mass, a raw base that looked like dirty candle wax. Then they carried this *pasta bruta* down the river to be further processed and purified.

A small percentage of the product stayed in Colombia as it moved along and stuck like splinters into the whores and junkies who built their homes from litter in the storm ditches of the steep towns like Medellín. Mostly, this was as crack cocaine, like little lumps of dirty salt for gritting roads that festered away under the skin of the people who got caught on it as it was transported by the FARC guerrillas across the border out of the country.

Most went through Mexico to the States, consumers of half the world's cocaine, about three hundred metric tonnes a year. The rest spilled out from the coast into the Caribbean, split into shipments by the cartels to find its way the four-and-a-half thousand odd miles over the Atlantic to the rest of the world. There are billions of pounds to be made from this.

Some travelled aboard coastal freighters that could carry two point five tonnes of the stuff, some carried by desperate crews on commercial fishing vessels. Sometimes, the shipment was slung beneath ships where it could be dumped if it had to be; there were even drug submarines now.

The consignments of drugs moved by a labyrinth of ways, in some cases even stuck by divers to the hulls of unwitting ships to travel like a parasite, the host remaining unaware; often, they were airdropped onto craft in the middle of the sea. Trying to find these things was like finding needles in a haystack.

The drugs would be retrieved and fed off to smaller boats that put to in coves and inlets too remote to properly police. And then they would come inland, to the receiving gangs, the wholesalers.

Broken down into diminishing packages the drugs spread out, finding passage in unnumbered ways, splitting up from the first conglomerate crop into parts ever smaller like the filaments of a firework until the tiny shrapnelled portions land home in some user and burn out. And trying to stop this thing is like trying to catch all the pellets from a cartridge. You have only a certain time in which to catch them after the charge is struck or the pattern gets too wide and they are gone into whatever bodies they will hit.

Some of those drugs came to the Scouser. When the system worked, it was as if the packets were hurled directly from Colombia into the waiting sack of his organisation. That was the word. Organised. This wasn't the formless violence of the street gangs. It was as organised as any other import business, an efficient set up with slick logistics. There were myriad little clowns out there playing out their hatreds against each other with no particular plan, but that was emotional. This was business. It worked on all the same principles, supply and demand, customer service, superior product, cost effectiveness, and paying the rent.

The Scouser had the restaurant, which could always launder money, could even explain with falsified takings the sudden boosts of income if the Scouser chose as he sometimes did to declare them. The webcam business provided another front, and his legitimate employee register made it easier to hide his key men, one highly paid as a computer technician, another as a chef, men more peripheral as waiters, barmen. All paying their stamp, staying off the social, appearing, on the outside, to be ordinary working citizens.

The girls were perfect couriers. While there were plenty of housewives earning a little extra money this way, his girls also worked on the streets, off the books,

123

and constantly brought in new customers.

The cockle-picking racket he'd started on the Wirral and that had since spread south put him in the perfect position to attract desperate men, and get a look at them physically. To pick his mules. People who were down on their luck, sometimes who shouldn't be here, people who were expendable, many already with criminal records who would work like red herrings if ever they were arrested, the police following the endless threads of their pasts back to all the wrong places, away from him. Not many dogs could smell cocaine through shellfish either, and from his base, the drugs fractalled out across the country.

It was growing and growing. As long as the organisation held, the sky was the limit. He just had to make sure he held it together. And the glue was fear.

Hold got the gun and checked it

over and took it apart and cleaned the barrel and re-oiled it, and wiped off the old oil where the cordite had mixed in. He wiped down the silencer and oiled the thread and put the whole gun back together again and again checked it. Then he stood it by the wall.

He went round the caravan with a wooden crate and put all the things he thought might matter into it and set it on the unit. He didn't quite know why he did that. Maybe he didn't want anyone else trying to decide what would have been important to him. Or maybe he just wanted to reduce himself right down, so there was nothing but the absoluteness of him going to do this. He went out to the van and got his driving licence and the superstitious five-pound note and put them in the box. What he told himself was that he did this so that all the things he cared about were in one place, so he could take them quickly if he had to.

He went back to the van and took down the rabbits and laid them on the grass then he got the old metal detector from the annex where he had put it and swung it over the rabbits and it registered nothing. There's no tracking device, he said.

He drove into town and paid a guy at the hardware shop ten pounds to unlock his mobile phone and then he took it back and put in the SIM card from the other phone and checked it worked. He'd asked, 'Is it possible to track a SIM card?' and said his mate and him had a bet. 'If you've got the hardware. Police can,' said the guy.

He smashed up the other phone and took it out and put it in an old wheelbarrow and poured in some petrol and lit it up. He thought of the pictures he was burning, as if each one of them burnt individually, like photographs, like they were some last possessions of the man. The phone curled foetally and he thought that he was burning some amnesia into the dead man, as if he had erased some thing the dead man could still be in touch with, could remember by.

If they can track the SIM card, they can track the SIM card. That's everything, he thought. That's everything I can do.

He went to the annex and unlocked

the gun cabinet and took out the shotgun and checked it and took it back to the caravan. He closed the orange curtains round the three sides of the living space and took his coat and propped it up with the rubber mop with its hood up like a man's head and set the table lamp before it so it looked like a man sitting from outside. Just the shape of him.

He took the box and put the rifle licence from the gun case in and his passport and took the shotgun and the rifle. Then he lay down in his clothes with the shotgun loaded and breached on his bed with him and the rifle rested against the wall.

Perhaps he was half asleep but something jolted him. He was up, the gun snapped shut, and swung, sitting, holding the gun at the open door. It was as if his senses followed him after the act. It was like some long borne device in him, some ancient spring reactant. Nothing moved.

He stood up and went from the room. The coat had fallen, the mop had clattered onto the floor. The need to sleep hit him again.

He turned off the table lamp and lay down on the long cushion in the living area. Then he breached the gun again.

Dream from childhood, absent for years, returning now at the beck and call of anxiety in his body. A lane of trees. The pheasant chicks he came across, a nine-year-old walking through lanes magnificent and bewildering to that child, between the ruined buildings of a farm netted with honeysuckle. Flycatchers clicking from boughs in their pretty ambushes. The roots, beside that collapsing, unused lane bursting from the fallen bank like branches of some backward trees searching for their light. And the child walks for the first time alone there, and there is the capacity for treasure in everything. And in that gone farm there is some sense of settlement, but he goes on.

In the darkening lane, the pheasant chicks. First, the lost, micking noise of them, then they are before him on the trail. And there is no discrepancy in their call, that peeped micking that is their lost attempt to be found. He tries to catch the chicks for their safety, and they scatter before him like a shoal of fish. One pheasant chick, the egg yellow, the dead bracken stripes upon it, smaller, left as the others bunch off the bank with peeping calls and are gone like blown seed. And now the child beneath the crowding pines recognises his part in this abandonment, in his need to intervene, and he tries to herd the chick, to undo this diaspora. All this was true, and truly happened, and the chick in its blind instinct ran into a hole. Like a bird hitting a window.

And he is that chick, as blind as silence; is in that passage of wet soil walls wherein he cannot turn himself around, in that tunnel of rats or snakes or some such things present or presently returning to come upon him there, as casual instruments of his fate. To stay or push on? Or else, within these tonnes of soil, sightless, he lies down and starves.

Once, he half woke. He lay waiting, half-real. Unfeathered, unfleshed, never found by rat nor snake, the perfect form of a bird, just the pile of bones in the tunnel.

He pushed sleep away like a weight

from him. There was the tiredness and the swelling of the battering and the ache of not sleeping in a bed and all the light was orange and unnatural round him through the curtains. It was like sleep had turned into something tangible, clung heavily to him like wet clothes.

He got up and showered with the gun next to him

and after he dressed he swallowed some pills and ate something and took the gun out to the annex and locked it up in the cabinet. 'What am I going to do with it?' he asked himself. 'What am I going to do? Shoot people?' He looked for a long time at the locked cabinet as if he was looking through it to the gun inside. Think of one thing. That's all you have to do. Just do one thing. There's no reason why they should hurt you.

He called and left a message with the man to say he wasn't well and that the pots should be okay; and that he would go out and bring them in tomorrow or the next day.

He'd waited a while, and then phoned Cara. Straight, flat-out lies. He said 'I didn't have a chill, I had a hell of a lot of fish. Hit this shoal. I had to keep going back and forth for the fish; I was knackered in the morning. Over eighty big fish. I don't want to tell him about it.' He could hear that part of her was excited for him. It would explain the cuts and bruises, the marks on him, if she saw them. And as he was speaking to her, something in him wanted overwhelmingly for her to look on his cut body. They could all be saved by this thing he was to do and he felt it could be the beginning of a new stage. If he got it right. He could say the bag kept cutting into me up the path. He could say he had to work partly with the tide coming in around him. Had wet feet, had to walk up and down like that. And he wanted very much that she would kneel and wrap his blisters as he was about to go and do this thing. And there was a great need in him to tell her everything about how he felt, as if the sides of the tunnel he had built had slipped and crashed into the water. Think of one thing, he kept saying. But think of one thing.

He said 'I'm going to take the fish up myself to the market, go direct.' He told the lies strongly and truly: 'I'm driving up to Liverpool to sell the fish. I should be back tomorrow.'

He took ice packs from the freezer that was in the annex and put them in the new coolbag and put the rabbits in and the bag would not close fully. He wished he'd slept more. My body got the rest, he thought. That's the important thing. I need to stay physically strong. He was aching from the battering of the rocks. It was my body that needed the rest. My mind is okay for now. He heard the words going round in his head, *prosser checkham. Checkham*. They were like a repetitive tune. In his tiredness he couldn't shake them out.

He went outside and looked out. 'Well,' he thought. He'd figured on four hours or so to the port. He put the box of things and the rabbits in the van. Then he locked up and went. He thought once more of the gun and thought no, don't take it. Then he drove.

They went out in the trawler to pick up an airdrop worth one point three million street and weighing around thirty kilos. It was the first time Grzegorz had been on a boat so small and the night was disorientating, felt spaceless. To the sides of the boat were strapped eight unpumped inflatables, and there were motors lined up on the deck.

The men crowded into the back of the boat and held variously on to the rails and the stanchions trying to find room amongst the motors. There was no sense of how fast they moved in the night, just this sound of progress, this persistent hiss through the water and the sound of the engine.

The men that had before been jocular and open were taciturn now, introspective. 'There's nothing to it,' thought Grzegorz. 'There's just driving the boat.' He watched the black line of the coast disappear, and watched until even the lights were too far off to see.

'*Mam nadzieję, że nie gniewasz się za bardzo.*' I hope you're not too angry he thought, about his wife.

The skin-headed Pole was up front with the crew and the pilot and one of the older men amongst them, in the back, spoke carefully.

'The throttle will be in your hand, like a motorbike.' He showed them surreptitiously on the motor by his legs. 'That's forward and reverse. That lever there. And those are the gears.'

The other men watched. They glanced now and then at the pilothouse and rode up and down with the boat.

'The sea will push you left, right and centre,' said the man. 'You just have to keep correcting. Follow the nose of the compass. You'll work out soon enough, but it goes the opposite way.' He shifted the tiller from side to side, looking up at the pilothouse. 'It's like reversing a trailer,' he said, 'it goes the opposite way to your steer.'

Every now and then the boat seemed to be making harder work through the water but when the man came out to talk to them about the way it would work, they seemed to be idling. Grzegorz was sure they were headed in circles. The cold had begun to bite them, even through the big puffer jackets they had. Grzegorz looked at his phone for the time. Harry spoke to him.

'*Nie ma totaj zasięgu.*'

'Nor me,' said Grzegorz. 'I don't have a signal either.'

The men watched in the trawler as the lights of the plane showed and heard the radio confirming the drop and saw the plane go over and the dark mass drop into the water. They rode the trawler to it and helped lift in the mass with gaff hooks by the netting it was covered with, and they stood back and watched the crew open the package and tear off the layer upon layer of hessian and polythene and watched as they measured the pack into smaller packages. It seemed to take forever.

As he watched, Grzegorz thought of his wife and the two sons and of the new life he could make with the ten thousand he would be paid.

They inflated the boats that were tied to the trawler and the generator on the boat was extraordinarily loud. They fitted on the motors with the heavy fuel tanks and extra fuel and took the packages they were given, and three miles from shore headed in to the different landing points they were allocated.

Most of the Poles had lied about handling a boat before. It was testament to the quality of their lies that they were entrusted with the packages. But then, there was the surety of their families. At the time Grzegorz was inflating the boat, his wife was up with their child who couldn't sleep and was asking for him.

They had electronic compasses and they had been pre-set to give the men bearings.

The men dispersed in the water and the trawler went off and there in the dark Grzegorz's compass failed. It was as simple as that. The software just froze.

He seemed to go for hours, hopefully. He headed the boat at the line of lights he could see way off in the distance, taking them to be the coast, but they were the scallop boats and when he had realised and turned away he was totally disorientated.

Hold drove to Cara's and looked at

the house. He knew she was at work. He looked at the knife on the front seat, some talisman, and said to himself that it would be enough. It brought some sense of something else to this.

He got out from the van with the box and took the key from its hanging place and went into Danny's shed. He saw the ambergris cutting, pinned up, faded, the triumphant men who had found it beaming from the picture, Danny's outside 'maybe'.

'What would you have done with this?' he said. 'Your "maybe" came in.'

He pushed the box of his things in at the back of a high shelf amongst rusted tins of paints and boat varnish. 'That's me,' he thought. 'They can do what they like to the caravan now. I don't care about anything else.'

He got back in the van. The new plastic of the coolbag stank on the passenger seat. He'd stopped for money and the roll of notes was curled up in the driver's doorwell. The phone was on the seat next to the bag and the in-car charger went umbilically from it to the lighter socket. 'Make sure you're near the phone. Get to the port. Wait.' Those were his instructions.

He looked at the rabbits in the bag and he thought of the man and he heard repeated the harrowing pleading of the woman's voice and thought of Cara sleeping in the room next to the boy that night and it

134

was as if only then he truly acknowledged that he had left one world. That how things had been would never come back to him. Things went cement just then. He looked out behind the house at the rising light.

He looked at the map, traced the red and green lines. 'Straight line,' he said to himself. 'It's just a straight line now.'

The big Irishman stepped outside

the pub and set his pint down on the sill and started methodically to roll himself a cigarette. It was a process which looked incongruous for him with his huge hands and yet he was deft at it and there was something almost childlike about it. It was barely mid-morning but a noise spilled out of the pub already.

The big man was about to light up when another man came out of the door with a phone in his hand looking for the big man. He gave the big man the handset and said 'Call...' just to say something and the big man waited with his hand over the mouthpiece until the man, who was the barman, had gone back inside. The phone looked like a toy in his hand.

'Yeah?'

Two other men were coming outside for cigarettes with pints in their hand and the big man looked at them and they nodded and went back inside.

'It's Stringer.'

'Stringer.'

'We've had the call.'

The big man waited for Stringer to talk things through. He listened while Stringer gave him the details, then he took the phone back into the pub.

Stringer had got the call first thing.

'No connection,' the man had said. 'Everything will be waiting for you, the usual way.' There was the hint of scouse accent.

'The taxi driver?'

The man made an affirmative noise down the phone.

'You want it quiet?' Stringer asked.

'No. Send a message.'

'How loud?'

'Very loud.'

Stringer understood.

Hold drove north. He tried to focus but he

was dogged with thought. He heard the child's voice on the phone, the almost birdlike greeting of *tato*. He had a picture of how old the boy was from the phone and hoped he was too young for this thing to register. He knew absolutely how it would be when *tato* did not come home.

His mother had drunk in darker moods before his father left, but it took a real grip once he went. It took Hold years to piece together the damage of that abandonment but as a child it washed over him straight away. His father simply didn't come home one day. All his mother's emotions seemed to collapse in on themselves; and while they mouldered inside her, the fruits of the fungus came out as great spores of blame. The abandonment somehow affected her worse than all his father's brooding moods. She blamed herself for not being able to lift them off him.

Hold was just at the wrong age. He was at the age where the sight of his mother in despair set off some heroism in him.

He wanted to be like Danny's father. He had strange mixed up feelings of relief that his father had gone, but he could not help the anger at the rubble it left of his mother and he dealt with that as he had learned to deal with everything else by then: to package things up tightly, to make a small solid thing of himself, something solid enough to support things.

He was Jake's age, thereabouts, when it happened. His father's act had been a wilful decision and Hold made a promise to himself – with the great affecting seriousness and belief of a child's promise – that he would never let people down that way.

It was only when he was older that he saw the drink take great lumps from his mother, thought

137

guiltily of how he would bring her glass after glass and feel somehow privileged at the smile she gave him.

He grew over-protective, perhaps, especially of his younger sister. She was out in Australia now. They hadn't really spoken for years. She said she couldn't cope with him being so protective of her, like he was throttling her. He blamed his father.

He wanted to make things right. He believed that you could sort things out; that you shouldn't give up on things. There was always a way. He felt that he had not been old enough to prevent his mother's drinking, hadn't understood it then; that he was wrong to be so protective of his sister; how perhaps the early baby was a way of screaming finally in his face that she could do what she pleased. He felt a great sense that he had got it wrong back then because he didn't know enough. It had just solidified into a haunting determination to do better. That had been the most crippling thing about Danny's death. That it could not be sorted out. But this was different. He thought of Danny and his belief in the impossible. 'Something will always come along. If you do things for the right reasons.' He had not believed in chance and Danny had, and here it was. He thought of their ambergris, the hallowed newspaper cutting, the one in a million find. This was it. Ambergris. Something had come along. And all he had to do was see it through.

He passed through the changing landscape,

noticed the rhododendron begin to grow loose on the hills, and he went on north. In amongst the evergreens, the bare deciduous trees had the silvery and papery look of wasp nests.

He thought of Danny's shed and then of the nest on the house. They had taken up the old floorboards, exposing the ceiling beams so you could see right through to the roof of the house. They piled the wood outside and watched the wasps strip the paper-fine layers off the boards with this repetitive, constant sound that seemed way too loud for something so small to make, gathering the pulped wood in their mouths.

While they rebuilt the annex they could hear the industry of the wasps crunching in the late spring warmth and they watched the small acorn of nest grow in the gable in the sun. All the time, this thing building that was dangerous and beautiful, but unnerving in its purpose.

By the time they had got the walls of the annex up the nest was as big as a football. When Hold went out there at night and stood below the nest he could hear it humming as the wasps fanned the warm air out of the nest with their wings.

'I want Jake here,' Danny said. 'I can imagine us all. Get that garden cleared. You have to have something to be doing things for,' he said. 'There has to be a purpose.'

I guess we didn't come far, thought Hold. We grew

up playing in that house and making up dreams in it, and we were still doing it in our thirties. He could feel the brick in his hand now, the weight of it, its roughness. The purposeful process of putting one brick down upon another. They've been the same for thousands of years, he thought. The size of a man's hand. That dictates everything – the size of the thing we can handle. What we can build like that.

'I want Jake here,' Danny said.

In the end, the great tits had taken to battering into the nest to knock the young grubs out. Then the magpies watched, learned, and just came in and hammered it down. All of that constructed because they were programmed that way. All that careful building and something just came along and battered it all down.

'I have to stay focused,' thought Hold. 'I have to stop thinking of things.'

For a while he considered throwing the rabbits and their dangerous guts to the side of the road, and of turning home. These thoughts are little tests of you, he said to himself. You know you have options. But he was haunted.

He couldn't stop thinking of the Polish woman. Of the distraught tone of her voice. He could picture her too clearly. His mother, Cara. It would be the same scene. The same collapsing. *Checkham. Vrooj prosser.*

140

Checkham, checkham. He thought of the dead man in the boat. It would be out of fuel by now, adrift again with the stiffened body. And then he saw the police car.

His stomach turned over. The car gained on him a few yards and then steadied, keeping a distance behind him.

Why were they out here? This was nowhere. Hold thought of the tyres, the brake lights, hoped nothing would draw attention to him. He drove carefully, but felt a nervous hesitancy on the corners that made him seem conspicuous.

They can't be here for you, he thought. It was like his thoughts were out loud. Why would they know? There's just the random chance they'll stop you. Why would they even look at the rabbits?

He looked at the mirror. There were two men in the car. I should stop, he thought. This is madness. Just stop and tell them everything. The possibility of it made him feel sick. Then they turned on the lights.

They'd timed it so that he could pull over easily into the lay-by that came up on his left and he fought this crazy urge to try and outrun them. He felt drained of focus. Give it up. This is your chance to get out.

He pulled the van into the stop and switched off the engine. 'Choose,' he said to himself. 'Choose now.'

The police officer knocked on the window and Hold wound it down.

'Afternoon, sir,' said the policeman.

Hold could sense the coolbag with the rabbits on the front seat.

'Hello,' he said.

'Do you mind stepping out of the car.'

Hold got out of the van and saw the other policeman checking the vehicle.

'Your van, sir?' asked the first policeman.

'Had her for years,' said Hold.

'And where are you off too?'

Hold veered. 'Can I ask why I've been stopped?'

'Oh. Just routine, sir. Just a check. Nothing to worry about, I'm sure. Full MOT?'

Hold nodded. The other policeman was checking the tyres.

'Mind if we take a look inside?'

It's your chance, right here, to give it up. You can end this now.

'No. On you go.'

The policeman nodded to the other policeman. 'Do you have your driving licence? Insurance documents on you?' The other policeman had opened the back and the doors squealed as he leant into the van.

'I don't, no.' Hold thought of the box on the shelf in Danny's shed, had a fleeting image of Cara finding them. Of his being jailed. 'They're at home.' *I can't let that happen. I have to get back to her.*

'Which is where, sir? Your address?'

Hold told him.

'And your name?'

Hold gave him the information.

'Any ID?' asked the policeman.

'No, not with me,' he said. Hold thought of the box again.

'I'll have to ask you to present your documents to your local station within seven days. Just routine, sir.'

'No problem.'

The other policeman came round with a handful of cartridges. 'You own a shotgun, sir?'

'Yes. Sorry. They must have come out of their box. I have a licence.'

The two police looked a little more thoughtful. You could see this cautious change come over them.

The one doing the talking got on the radio and radioed the information in, asking about the driver and the shotgun licences.

You can tell them. You can tell them now, thought Hold. He waited while the voice through the radio came back with the information. There was this static squeak. The other officer was going round again kicking the tyres.

'Where did you say you were headed?' asked the policeman.

'To a friend.' Hold picked a place out of the air, hoping it was far enough from them.

'What's the address?' The policeman had the notebook out and was waiting for the address.

'I don't know,' said Hold. 'I couldn't tell you.' He made this huge gamble. 'I could drive you there, but I've no idea of the actual address.'

Hold thought of his box of things on the shelf. Had a vision of Cara finding them. Had a vision of him having achieved nothing more than turning himself into a greater burden to her, a dead weight in jail she would feel tied to. The policeman looked at him and closed the notebook.

'We'll need you to present your gun licence along with your other documents, when you take them in,' he said.

'Of course,' said Hold. He could feel his pulse smash in his chest now, hoping it didn't show all over him.

The policeman leant into the window.

'Shoot those yourself, did you?' said the police, nodding at the rabbits on the seat.

'Two-two,' said Hold. 'Not a shotgun.'

The policeman nodded as if he understood. There was this rich stream of adrenaline through Hold like he had too much blood.

You've chosen. Right there. That was it. You cannot consider any doubt anymore.

'Well, thank you for your cooperation, sir. You can go on your way.'

'That's fine,' said Hold. 'Have a good day.'

He got in the van and started the engine and waited for the police to drive off but they flashed him on.

He let a car go past and pulled out and they pulled out behind him and stuck to him again as if they were waiting for him to slip up. He could see the one not driving on the radio.

'They know,' he thought. 'They're going to stop you again. They're just waiting.' Then they closed in on him and overtook, and disappeared ahead on the straight.

'Why? Why did I make this choice?'

Grzegorz thought. But he knew. 'I know why I made this choice. You always have to wait in line. All my life I've been waiting in line. Wait your turn, know your place. That's all there is. I wanted to change something.'

Grzegorz held the compass in his hands and pressed the buttons uselessly. He was totally and absolutely lost on the utter pitch darkness of the sea. Only the compass screen glowed, with this factual light. He felt the urge to cry, like a distant need he still associated with childhood. He felt defiant little angers in him. He felt pricks of hope. Fear. But he could not hold on to any of them, not on to one single emotion. Then it was like he shut his eyes to them.

The sun had seemed to drop quickly.

He waited with the others outside the gates. He had just come off shift, had peeled off the once white overalls, now, by the end of shift, plastered in blood and tissue. It was cold outside the gates, but a different cold from the deliberate cold inside of the abattoir where the fresh blood was like warm water on his hands and he welcomed that warmth.

Had he known then, waiting there, smoking, that it would come to this? Had he, underneath, the under-standing of this? He had felt it. He had ignored it. He had jumped off the bridge.

The sweat dried on his body and he felt the cold go. He thought of the different types of cold, the cold of the fields at home that was so complete it was almost imperceptible until you felt your bones ache, your teeth throb. He thought of the salt-laden cold of the bracing space of the beach, the cold gritty sand between his fingers, the sense of the slow vast fridge of water. Even the way the gulls were coloured, in grey shades.

'I have to stop thinking of the cold,' he told himself. He had one or two cigarettes and he lit one.

'They bullied me, but that was fine,' he thought. 'It's not my reason for doing this. I can't pretend it is. I just had this hope, that's all. They didn't drive me to this.'

The small sepal of the boat showed up in the glow of the indrawn cigarette.

He thought of fires as a child. There were always fires. He thought of the great stack of dirty straw smoking in the field, the smell of it drifting on the subdued autumn breeze.

146

'I couldn't have stayed,' he thought. 'A man has to try to improve things.'

He finished the cigarette. He felt nothing now. The problem had stopped feeling real. He was at that stage when he believed he had overreacted. Maybe it was the cigarette. It just brought a little calmness. He threw it into the sea and the pitch blackness came around him again.

He took the compass out from inside his puffer jacket where he'd put it to warm, thinking it might have frozen in the cold.

'Can electricity freeze?' he wondered. He had this picture of lightning coming down into the stubble fields, the glorious momentary frozenness of it, the whitening of the air around.

The compass's square of clinical light was mesmerising, hypnotic, the only point of reference in the dark. He used the luminance torchlike to look for anything that might work to press within the tiny reset hole. There was nothing. There was just nothing on the boat.

'Your friend talked to you?'
'Yes, he talked to me.'
'You want the work?'
He'd nodded.
'How much did he say? How much did he tell you?'
'Everything, I think.'
He'd been momentarily distracted by a cloud of

147

egrets that lifted off the beach and flew strangely away,
their necks folded. They didn't seem to fit there in that
place, seemed too beautiful, like some anomaly.

'He told you of the risk?'

'Yes.'

'Your family?' The man had repeated the requirements.

Grzegorz looked down at the compass, sure the
light was fading, sensing in his hand the battery
draining out. He thought of the passivity of the cows,
going to the stun plate.

'I understand...'

They watched the trucks come in. As they waited for
the driver to pick them up, a long lorry packed with
lambs came through and went in through the big zinc
gates and as they passed, Grzegorz saw the stubborn,
incomprehensible eyes. They were mad, somehow.

'I understand.'

A little way down the road he stopped

again. The adrenaline of the police stop had rolled up
in him and he felt queasy, travel-sick almost. He'd gone
through the quarry towns, set precariously in amongst
the banks of scree, and there was something megalithic
in them, some sense of his own smallness as the
mountains grew bigger. He felt tiny against them, and
against the massive industry man was capable of.

I should have left something for Cara, he thought. What if I don't get back? He felt that he was drawing all his sentiments and knowledges of this thing from some Sunday afternoon Western now, over-dramatising it. It did not feel real. With the tiredness and the driving and the ebbing adrenaline, everything suddenly became surreal in one gutting flash, and he felt absolutely out of his depth and angry about being given this chance. How could he turn away from it? Everything was at stake now. It had been delivered up to him and given him the possibility of things.

He felt dizzy and stopped the van, pulled up into a gateway. Like some chasm, the valley and the dark lake sat before him. He got out of the van and stared down into this drop, this void. He had a vision of himself angry, saw himself scream and smash things, had this great feeling for the need for release. The phrase was going over and over in his head. *Checkham. Prosser checkham.* You stupid boy, he thought. You stupid, stupid boy. But still he couldn't beat out the phrase that was becoming like a little song in him, as if the packets were calling somehow.

I could go into a hotel or a supermarket or somewhere, there are loads of foreign workers here now. I could find someone who might talk the language. I don't want to draw attention to myself though. You can't just go round asking questions of strangers. Stay focused. It doesn't matter what it means.

149

The wilderness seemed to gape at him, beckon open-mouthed at him like some great animal. He pictured hurling the rabbits and their dangerous guts into this maw, pictured turning round and heading home. He wanted so much to convince himself this was for some purpose all of his own, so he could walk away from it, lift his eyes up from it. He tried to drag Cara out of the reason for this, tried to disbelieve it was the Polish woman's fault. Who was she anyway? A criminal's wife. An immigrant. He couldn't do it. He couldn't raise the hate.

He thought of the voice on the phone, of the child and of the baby and he felt very clearly how it would be for them now. *Vrooj prosser checkham.* He thought of the words, they started to ring in his head again. And he thought of the threat to them that had been made and thought, 'No, I cannot throw these packets away now. It's almost as if they have some kind of life of their own, that they are making a demand.' In his decisiveness, he was trigger finger, barrel and bullet all, and the ridding himself of these packages came to him only as fantasies, as things possible to a man who had not yet made this decision. 'I am doing this thing now,' he repeated. Once you pull the trigger, you are responsible for everything that happens in the path of that bullet. You can get all the way to having something in your sights and you can still back out. But if you do pull the trigger, you're up. You follow it through. You can't call the bullet back. 'Don't put this on her,' he said. 'Don't make this some moral thing.' It wouldn't be a get out to say you'd done it because they had been threatened. 'This is part of your choice.' It would make a difference to them though, perhaps, if they knew. If they knew he didn't just abandon them. That perhaps he was doing something he thought would help things. He ought to give them that.

He got back in the van and sat there. He sat there and looked at his hands on the steering wheel, looked at the raising welt on his thumb where the skin was reddened and had started to gather a small reservoir of · pus. 'It's just the ignorance of it that's scaring you,' he said. 'It's that you don't know about it. You had your chance to get out just then with the police and you didn't even really consider it. You just have to stop thinking it's a cowboy film. Nothing's going to happen.'

He looked at the rabbits in the bag on the seat next to him and felt as if there was a hum coming from the packets, some sinister, persuasive beat. He thought of the house renewed. He thought of Cara and Jake. Had this picture of them settled. Of dangerous hope. He threw this back like a little mechanism to make himself go on. *If you can do this, if you've got the balls for this, then you've got the balls to say you want her.*

'Just don't lose your nerve,' he thought. 'Just hold your nerve, now.'

Grzegorz thought about the details

he had solemnly handed the man about his wife and children and tried for hours with the compass until he eventually hurled it into the night and screamed and beat the boat, thinking of his family.

He thought of his wife this morning, the passive tired want in her eyes as he left for work and she queued for the bathroom with the babies. He had wanted to hold her, tell her, but he couldn't. Not just because he couldn't tell her of the job he was to do, but from habit too. They had fallen out of the habit of touching each other. He seemed to have grown this shell on himself, but it felt not like something which had grown from within, but like the outside around him had stuck on to him, somehow. Covering him up, like being buried alive.

She just stood in the queue and he left, confused at himself, confused at the faint, exhausted distance to her now. He felt she'd got to a point of carelessness. 'I came with you,' she seemed to say. 'You promised me things and you didn't bring them to me.'

It was not gone though. He knew that. Whatever the brittleness between them in the day, there was a sad softness in the night. Something automatic, beyond them. It was the place. The situation was the problem and it had been he who brought them here, brought them here away from her mother and sisters, and she had followed because she believed in him.

'Jest mi zimno.

'Boję się.

'Jestem spragniony.

'Jestem głodny.'

I am cold. I am scared.

I am thirsty. I am hungry.

He thought of her softness and it gave him a great, angry hopelessness.

'Mam nadzieję, że nie gniewasz się za bardzo.'

'I hope you're not too angry,' he thought again. 'I had to try.'

Eventually, he ran out of fuel and partially refilled the tank but did not know he had to prime the fuel through and so the boat just started drifting.

That far out Grzegorz had no signal on his phone. He had not told his wife what he was doing and she did not know where he was. When the drift brought him within a mile of the coast the messages began to come through. Some of them had hung in the air waiting for the phone for days. At one point so many messages came through that the phone seemed to flash. By then, without food or water and with the extreme cold, Grzegorz Przybylski was dead.

Snow still lay in the shadows of the hillcrests but Hold looked down onto the difficult roads and drove carefully and with focus the way cut through this rubble and monumental ancientness until he crossed the water onto the sudden flatness of the island, the mountains rising behind him as if they were closing him in to some great amphitheatre.

The road opened into easy dual carriageway, seemed to offer movement through the scoured scene powdered with gorse and new lambs. He had the sensation of being cast towards the place, as if let from an open hand after the bunched fist of the mountains. A dice rolled onto a table.

As he drove, a beetle worked its way along the dashboard. It was tiny, jewel-like in the light that got through the windscreen, itself like some piece of crushed glass.

Hold kept his eyes on the road but all the time they were drawn to the tiny beetle, smaller than his fingernail.

The beetle walked industriously around and travelled down the face of the panel and stopped, sensing the moving draught through the air vent. It turned and headed back up the slope, then opened its wing cases in its mechanical looking way and it went up into the air with the faintest hum and clicked clumsily against the windscreen.

It doesn't matter where you try to go, thought Hold. You're in this van now, and you're going where it's going, whatever you do inside the space of it.

The tiny beetle worked along the inside of the screen, and went out of sight.

For a moment his stomach turned at the sign for a vehicle checkpoint until he drove past another saying that the checkpoint was closed, and more distinct in the March light as he approached it, there was the lump of Holy Island. The checkpoint sign had set the word in his head again, *checkham, checkham*.

As he drove over the causeway to the port a flock of curlews lifted over the wall and cut across above him and disappeared into the thin marsh at the side of the road and he remembered the strangeness he felt on the cliffs. This great split in his life had come within that strangeness, and it was as if they were some sign.

Over the causeway he came into the mouth of the town. After the long, straight drive it was a kind of shock. The busyness of the signage and the choices to make almost caught him out.

There was something beckoning and mesmeric about the way to the dock but he bore left into the town with this uneasy feeling of nervous avoidance he didn't understand fully. Then the idea of the police and the customs officers at the port sat up in him like something remembered suddenly and he thought of the rabbits and their vital insides. That was it, he thought.

155

That was what is strange about the land here. The whole place looks like it's been cropped by rabbits.

After the busyness and internationalism of the roads that went off to the port, Hold expected the town to be bigger and he seemed immediately to be headed up out of the place almost as soon as he'd turned into it. The houses and shops around him were rough and hard and salty looking.

He went up a short climb out of what must have been the heart of the town and parked. He was uneasy. 'Come on, focus,' he thought. He thought the town would be bigger and hold an anonymity for him but he felt exposed already. He parked up feeling that the van drew attention to him. 'It is what it is,' he told himself. 'You can't make assumptions.' Everything seemed to be private houses, people's homes. A place people worked, he thought, not a place people fed off. The sort of place people get noticed. It had a mixed up oldness and newness, a kind of utility to it.

He saw a sign for Ucheldre and knew he was in the high part of the town. He took the things he needed from the van and put them into the small bag and shouldered it and went to the parking meter then came back and put in the ticket and took up the bag of rabbits and looked around for the way into town.

He walked away from the van and looked back at it as if checking to see it looked anonymous and he realised that he was tired now from the driving. He

156

could feel this warm, comfortable spring sun on him like a little gift. He put his coat over the rabbits, hiding them in the bag that wouldn't close.

'It's fine,' he thought. 'You need to relax.' He could feel the weight of the rabbits and the kilo of drugs and looked around and tried to get some sense of the place, of the layout. Then he followed the signs into town.

His mind drifted. It seemed to come into colour, warmed by the sun, like a scent lifting. He thought of the drugs being tracked and remembered the metal detector all over again and thought of the time Danny had hidden things and of the brooch, and then of the time Danny had got some shark's teeth from a souvenir shop and hidden them around. 'Rare as hen's teeth,' he had said to the boy. 'I bet you could find some hen's teeth if you looked, as long as you believed in them,' and he gave Jake ten pence for each one he found. 'I guess he never stopped believing in treasure, Danny,' thought Hold. 'I guess none of us really do.'

He walked into the centre of the small town to the pedestrian area and was startled again by the market, as he had been by the choice of roads. He felt over aware of the bag he carried, he felt watched. 'You can't be,' he said. 'They don't know you. They don't know who you are. Just be natural,' he thought. It was like he existed in a kind of pod.

He crossed the pedestrian area, passed the closed

157

Woolworth and followed the natural draw downhill and went through an alleyway onto a new bridge and over the road. It was odd, this beautiful bridge against the wasted buildings of the town.

He stood for a while in the sun on the new incongruous bridge watching the cars beneath on the road, trying to get a sense of the place all the time; then he headed over the bridge, over the railway tracks and the still span of enclosed water to the ferry complex on the other side. There was this reassuring salt smell off the bay.

'I could just go,' he thought. 'Nobody knows about Cara and Jake. I could just go.' He looked out, feeling the calm sense of the water and he was unused to feeling this in a town. This wasn't his environment. He did not have a natural understanding of it, how to fit into it, but he felt the sense of the water and of the sun. 'No,' he said. He looked back at the dirty town buildings by the road. 'I don't have my passport. Do I need a passport for Ireland? You wouldn't go anyway. Stop thinking the thing. You're just going to see this through.'

He went in to the Tourist Information Office and found some maps, a town guide.

'Would you like any help?' the girl asked pleasantly but it was strange in the nasal north Walian whine.

'No, I'm fine,' Hold said. 'I don't need anything.'

The place was full of Welsh dragons and fudge. He

158

looked at a rack of postcards, jokes, women in stovepipe hats. All these clichés. 'Maybe I should let her know,' he thought, thinking of Cara. He did not articulate the thought in his own mind: in case I don't come back. 'That's a cliché too,' he thought. 'Stop thinking like you're in some cowboy film.' He felt like he needed a conversation with himself. 'Just get it done,' he said.

He went out of the Information Centre and walked back towards the bridge. 'I have to know this place,' he thought. He felt this need for proactivity. 'I have to get to know this place.' He checked the phone with a sudden thought that he might have somehow missed a call, or not have a signal. *No. It was fine.* He looked for a while at the train lines and considered how the meeting would happen, where the men would come from. Then he went back over the bridge.

The thickset redhead stood in the station by the information boards with the black leather sports bag cradled on the floor between his feet. He stood under the panelled glass roof staring up at the great structure of the strut work and held the cardboard cup full of coffee.

The station throbbed and rushed with people. Some scallies were shouting and pranking over by the palm trees that grew surreally inside the station and two uniformed police stood there tiredly watching. The man thought of the bag between his feet and imagined he could sense a heat off it. The scallies were shouting and yelping formlessly. They all wore hoods and looked the same. You could tell what the police wanted to do. He wanted to do it himself. He imagined cracking their heads together in an effective way. Time was when he would have done, maybe even the police would have, but not now. Now it was all business.

He watched the crowd, imagining himself stepping down the aisle to the centre of the hall, climbing into the ring, all these people here to watch him, his name announced. 'If it wasn't for this nose,' he thought. He saw himself spit blood carelessly into the basin and held the coffee cup to his mouth with two hands, as if it had a spout to drink through. Left, right, left, left, right. 'If it wasn't for this nose,' he thought. He'd moved on from the scallies, and in his mind they were big opponents, and he was laying them out, one by one, to the cheers of the crowd.

He felt the three bleats of his phone in his pocket and picked up the black sports bag and went out to the drop-off point and over to the taxi that was pulled up. He got in and put the bag on his lap. The car filled up with the smell of the coffee. The driver nodded. He had a strange face like a dieting owl. He'd met him before. It was the boss's man at the port. Always a taxi driver, wherever they were. It was a simple and clever way of getting under things.

'You're clear on what to do?'

The owlish man nodded, and the thickset redhead got out, leaving the black sports bag on the seat.

He got out of the car and he was stepping from the limo, a girl on either arm. They were like models. Sequined dresses. The flash bulbs crashing off like a firework celebration, wearing the sharp dinner jacket and the heavy belt about his waist like a cummerbund.

He walked into the station to meet his crowd again and behind him the owlish man drove off. The redhead was holding the cup as if it was a mic. 'My nose held up,' he told the reporters, 'I had to protect it, but I kept it clean and it held up.'

They pulled up in the car and Stringer went up and knocked at the door and the big man's mother opened it. In his long black coat, Stringer had a look of priest-like officiousness, of a finicky clerk. It was a thing for him to try to dress well after growing up where he did, like hiding a damp bit of wall with a painting.

'Good afternoon, Mrs Gleeson.' He beamed. The smile didn't suit Stringer's face. It made him look odd, like a man wearing the wrong hat.

161

The big man appeared behind his mother in the corridor of the small house. He was dabbing at his mouth with a napkin with the same strange deft way he had rolling the cigarettes.

'Will you come in, Declan? And your friend,' asked the mother.

'I think we're ready to go,' he said. She looked past Stringer at the driver in the car. You could just see him through the window, scratching at his red face.

'Get away! You just go back and finish your tea there, Galen.' The big man looked bashfully at Stringer. 'You can't work without your tea.'

The big man went through back to the kitchen and Stringer followed him in. There was no arguing with her.

'Will your friend not come in?' said the mother.

'No,' said Stringer. 'He's fine.' He wanted to say: 'He's not house-trained.' He had this thing against the lower ranks.

'Will you have some food?'

'No, thank you Mrs Gleeson,' said Stringer. He was swallowing these big bags of impatience and he thought of the driver waiting in the car. He studied the woman trying to work out how she could produce such a thing as the big man. Then he looked down at the big man's plate. 'It'll be the food,' he thought. There was a pile of boxty and the grotesque looking stew. Stringer glued this ridiculous smile on, like a salesman.

'Will you not even have a cuppa?'

'No, thank you, Mrs Gleeson. We ought to be going.' He looked daggers at the big man. He was wolfing the huge plate of food. He couldn't eat any quicker.

'Don't you rush,' said his mother. 'You'll get the wind. I've not made your sandwiches yet.' She was busy with the bread and the stuff on the unit. It was like she was under some sort of automatic order to feed things.

'Will you want some sandwiches too, there, Declan?'

'No,' said Stringer.

'There's plenty here.'

He pulled himself up. 'No, thank you Mrs Gleeson.'

Stringer could feel the time peeling away. He sat and stared nastily at the big man and looked round the room. There was the sound of the mother making sandwiches. Stringer thought of the trip ahead. He understood the need to keep up the pressure of fear and the engine that had to drive that. His devoted little furiousness at it came mostly from the stupidity of people. They knew the score, why did they have to test it? The engine was relentless. You just did not get away with it, it couldn't be allowed, so why did they test it? That was what he did. He kept the machine oiled.

He looked around the warm little room. There were pictures of the two boys, the other one much

163

more normal sized, much more his size, more natural to the woman he thought. There was a picture of the woman's late husband, and an Irish flag in the corner. Stringer felt this pang of jealousy at the pride in the house. He felt a jealousy at the familial love it represented. He didn't understand this Catholic thing. He'd always felt like an outsider to it. He'd like to have grown up here, not on the dingy, hungry street he did. Here and there around the place were silly little shamrock ornaments and leprechauns. Against that, the big man was like some big overgrown child.

Hold walked out over to the marina,

the water calmed inside the vast breakwater truly seagreen, settled.

The beach was strange to him sitting against the town because the town had a strange spread out look here. He took it in, Thin shores of white, flinty pebbles. A low howl across the water he could not place at first, eerie, that seemed to be some premonitory message from the sea beyond the break.

'I have to keep a feeling of strength now,' he told himself. 'Keep that strength, that feeling of strength. Just concentrate on holding that.' He thought of it as something he was carrying, that he couldn't put down however heavy it got.

He looked out, onto the mainland and the mountains, could see the clouds smudging up with a later promise of rain. He knew the sort. It would be flat, light rhythmic rain, and it would come over, almost like a tired patch, later in the afternoon.

He looked at the breakwater a while then walked a little way further and sat and put the bag with the rabbits down beside him and pushed it with his foot out of the sun under the bench. He looked absently at the plaque on the bench, *in memory*. He thought of someone who must have loved to sit and watch this view. It has to happen somewhere public, he thought. Somewhere like this.

He looked down at the sore on his thumb, lifted now and raised into an angry welt. He pushed at it with the finger and thumb of his other hand and it swelled with tension. The pain was sharp and small and focused and he picked at the top of the welt with his rough thumbnail until the skin split. The ring of buttermilk pus gave through the skin with a minute breaking of tension, and the splinter lifted in the fluid and spilled out onto Hold's hand. He picked it up. He rubbed the pus and the pink water off his hand and looked at the shard. Brick. It's brick from the house, he thought.

He turned round and took in the one mountain, rising strangely out of the flat ground of the island. That would be a good place to get to, to get an idea of the land, he thought. It won't happen there though. It has to be somewhere like this. He turned back and scanned the promenade, wiped his hand clean again and flicked the splinter of brick out at the beach. Here, the bluish rock was igneous and looked liquefied, twisted under geology's great pain rather than snapped like the rocks on the beach he was used to.

The watery pus was running a little on his hand and he stared at it, this repellent stuff from inside himself. He could have no idea where this thing would be. He could not second guess them. Why would it be different from selling anything else? I have what they want. If it falls to me to pick it, I'll pick somewhere like this. Somewhere exposed. Somewhere where I'm in sight of people. He fought the urge to get up and go down to the beach and put his hand in the water.

They sat in the car and went off,

the red-faced man driving them out past the tidily careful small gardens. In the back, Stringer felt the little hatred again, a strange despising jealousy at the tame houses. He felt there was a kind of ridiculous Easter egg prettiness to them. It had riled him, being called Declan. He was Stringer to everyone now. But something was always there, bringing you back to what you were, not letting you move on. It was humiliating. A wagging finger.

They went on into the inner city. Instantly the slow urban traffic thickened and Stringer cursed. They had time before the ferry, but he hated to put the simple parts of a thing in jeopardy, like getting to the ferry on time to get the tickets, to take stock. I'm a professional, he thought. That mostly means not getting the simple bits wrong.

'This goddamned traffic,' he said out loud. They ground into it and stop-started. He had this nervous energy and he hated to stay still.

'I hate to be cooped up. That was the worst thing about the stretch,' he thought. He seethed and felt this anger come up. For him it was like some weird beast from outside. 'That's it. That's it right there.' He was angry even at his own anger. 'If it wasn't for that I'd have been out in half the time. But that culchie deserved it.' He remembered melting the blade into the toothbrush handle, the way the plastic choked and bubbled like something lunar and seemed to paste itself into the razor to hold it fast.

'You couldn't take that lip off someone and not do something about it. He deserved it,' Stringer told himself. 'That culchie. He shouldn't have pushed me.'

Stringer looked out at the streets. The people moving on them were bizarre colours against the cement. It was turning back into a dirty city, Stringer could feel it. Now the money was leaching away, the services were being sucked out like suds down the plughole of an emptying bath. The litter was collecting, the dog shit. The stones layering again with a mild soot. Just the colourful corner pubs were there, men smoking outside them. We got treated to a health spa, that's all. It was just a visit. He felt a cruel joy at that.

'I should have got some kind of promotion, for keeping my mouth shut. I should have been fast-tracked when I got out. I deserve more than this, doing clean-up jobs with this big monkey. They got seven years head start on me, those others, and they left me behind. Seven years out while I was sitting around keeping my mouth shut. Just like getting stuck in traffic. Well, I've got brains of my own. I'm tired of this. Stuck in traffic. I deserve a chance to make something of myself,' he thought. He fell to staring out of the window, a kind of heavy glass-like quality to him.

Hold was of singular purpose now.

Some strong thing in him felt as if he could see those things before him that were about to come, but at the same time he felt this as a paper shadow, and that at any time that feeling of strength could blow down.

He thought back to home. He thought of Cara's freckles, the secret freckles on her shoulders, and felt, in fact, a great brotherly love for her. He imagined Jake in the house, the sun coming in through the window of the new bedroom, the attic room where they'd had their den, he and Danny.

He imagined a busyness of men there, working on the house, the garden cleared, his hands stained with soil as he put in the shrubs and dug out the old borders. He wanted very much to have, at the end of this, the sense that he had done something complete, and turned someone's life around.

'Where will I go,' he thought. 'I don't care, I can't answer that. I'd like a small place right up the valley, and a boat.' He laughed gently at himself. 'It won't be enough for that. It won't be enough for any of it, but it's a start. It will secure the place and give us a start. Maybe I could get a boat though, start getting the money in for myself.' He felt wistful, thoughtful, philosophical. As if the determination was safe in him now.

He looked at the great ship sitting there at the terminal and had this picture of departure, what it must take to leave a thing. 'Is that harder in the end than sticking with it?' he thought. 'No.' He thought of his father. 'No, following things through is harder. Keeping at them. Or maybe it's just how we're geared,' he thought. 'We get to be a way, after a certain time, and we can't be any other way however much we try.'

There are hundreds of driving forces, just another one of which is the desire to provide. And this was Hold. He could no more have walked away from the beach empty handed than years ago refused his mother a drink. And in him too was a great sense of guilt at anything he took for himself. It was his will to provide without taking. It was, in a way, a form of self-harm. He had missed that vital stage where we learn that we must be able to allow others to know that we take from them.

He thought of the Pole's wife and family and how they must have come on some big boat or plane like that but he did not think of them in any sad way. He thought of them just in the way that they were part of this thing, now – that everything was. That there was this massive great world out there and men were just the little things of what happened in it and that there was no difference between them and him or everyone else involved in this and that it was just some big process that he could or could not have set into motion, and he'd chosen to do it. Now here they all were.

He watched for a while a mother and child throw bread to a gaggle of ducks that gathered 'chocking' on the prom. 'I didn't choose that,' he thought, looking at the simple happiness of the mother and child. 'I chose not to have that.'

He walked out past the boat store, looking back to the parked, restive ferries at their terminal, and stood a while looking out across the bay. There were one or two people working on their boats, where they stood propped on the hard ground, and the smell of paint and anti-foul drifted to him. The breeze licked in, and a pasty green weed skinned the rocks flattening out into the still water. Faintly, someone had a radio on and within that noise he placed finally the low howl, the hollow mewl of the wind through the masts seeming to amplify the little breeze.

He looked out at the sea. I need that. I need that the sea is there, he thought, looking over the water. I need the knowledge of the presence of this. Sometimes it doesn't look real. It is important. I cannot imagine being away from it. It seems impossible that we can exist at the same time as it.

Hold looked at a big new fishing boat. It was fresh with paint and the paint caught the sun with a wet look it was so fresh. Even the railings and the metalwork reflected, so new was it that it hadn't been in the water yet, and the salt hadn't mottled the zinc into a white, stone-like look.

The idea of the ownership of it came to him surreally, gave him a sense this was all strange, dream-like.

'I wonder how much she'd cost,' thought Hold.

He walked on, taking a path he thought would follow the coast, checking now and then that he still had a signal on his phone. He wanted to walk, felt he could walk for days.

Around him the gorse warmed and smelled of coconut. He was thinking of the new boat and, for some reason, fresh paint on the old house window frames and the suddenness of the place he came to took him by surprise, a strange dishevelled overgrown space. It just didn't feel real, as if he was thrown into some kind of film again.

It looked like an old hotel, some abandoned edifice once grand, a Hollywood set somehow reasonless here. Its windows were shut up with blocks and graffitied over, like strange mascara on its eyes. There was a wonderment to it, a surrealness, as if someone had fixed up a backdrop. Something in him had this weird sentiment that this was where it could happen, referred back again to the sense he couldn't help feeling, that all this was just a film.

Hold could feel his focus blurring. He had this odd sense of things being put in place around him. 'It's just a surprise,' he said. 'It's just a surprise to find it here.' Rabbits scattered, and there was evidence of them everywhere. There was something human and physical about the place, something in the curled hair of dead bracken that lay across the slope. As if the whole place wanted to stand up and pour its heart out.

He went up the tumbled steps that seemed to be of marble and stood in the space before the house on the broken shells and bits of coloured glass scattered there in the grit. It played with his sense, as if he had fallen out of another time here. Looking at the broken glass he thought again of the beetle that had been caught in the van. The tiny, reflective colour of it. I could have put it out, he thought. I could have stopped and put it out.

Around the place was a busted garden. Fingers of escaped rhododendron went supplicant into the sky from the dying grass and limbs of trees were rolled into half-burned fires long out, as if some effort of clearing had been made once and then been given up because the place itself had refused the help. A lone iron streetlamp stood there, bewildering somehow in the shrinking space.

He walked on unnerved and followed a rough track out onto a wooden jetty and looked back into a muddy bay and the hulk of a wrecked boat in it, behind it a strange building like a toy castle, some unreal film backdrop again. He looked at the red boat and its muted reflection in the thin water and the gorse growing on the bank behind it. He knew inside that he had no notion of how to do this thing he was about to do, nor of this place he had come to, no sense of it.

He walked down onto the little beach of mud where the wreck sat disproportionate and turned onto the road back into the town. He passed a house, a child's swing rope in the garden. It looked in that light like a hangman's noose. In his hand he realised he held some pebbles he had reached down for absently, as if he had needed some hard reality, some contact with the earth. He held them in his hand, blued and shot with quartz, glistening and powdered with fool's gold that was like a dust in them.

He looked at the fool's gold and remembered the piece of shale he'd left for Jake, thought of the muddy smell of shale in the rain.

'I have no idea here. I have no idea what will happen now.'

The big man sat with the pile of sandwiches on his lap and after a while he started to eat them.

'You want one?' he asked Stringer.

'No,' said Stringer.

'You want one?' he asked the driver. The driver was scratching the eczema on his face absently. 'Yes,' he said, to the sandwiches.

'There's cheese, tuna paste, or corned beef,' said the big man. 'What do you want?'

'I don't know. Surprise me,' said the driver.

The big man passed a sandwich over without looking, like it was a nice game, and they went along stopping and starting in the traffic, the driver and the big man eating the sandwiches.

'These are good sandwiches,' the driver said. He had the kind of strange slowness of his body that people who drive a lot have.

For the big man this was like a day trip. He chewed at the sandwiches, getting the paste stuck up in his teeth, and looked out at the city, as if he'd never seen it this way, by being driven round in a car, before. It was still a low city and let a lot of light in. He had this small excitement going on at the idea of the boat, and had it all down pat in his head.

'You going over for long?' asked the driver. The big man started to answer.

'Why ask?' said Stringer from the back, sharply.

'Nothing, Stringer, just talking. Sorry.'

The big man saw the driver's face go extra red and felt guilty for it, like it was his fault, going to answer the question. He felt sorry for the driver seeing the heat go up in him. The driver was the kind of guy you could tell had a family, thought the big man. There was a kind of scared domesticity to him, and Stringer knew it and preyed on it, like he preyed on the big man for being less smart than him. There was this ticking unpredictability coming off Stringer in the back, this kind of fermentation. It made a horribleness in the car.

'That's Mister fucking Stringer,' Stringer said in this way, under his breath.

They pulled to a halt behind the continually stalling traffic. Around the entrance to the pub they were alongside men were busily going in and out. It was restless, like at the hatch of a beehive.

'You want another sandwich?' said the big man. He was trying to restore things. It had been okay before in the car, eating the sandwiches.

175

The driver looked cowed. 'No,' he said. It was like it had spoiled everything. 'Nah.'

The big man felt deflated. He sat back in his seat and stared out of the window. He watched a kid dodge through the traffic, banging needlessly on the bonnets as he wound through the slow cars. Mildly, the big man remembered the last job. It was just a battering. A soft lesson. That kid's legs were tucked in his socks, and he wore a baseball cap, just the same as the one he was watching go through the traffic. There were always these knackers to put down. 'It's like they didn't get the lessons,' thought the big man.

He remembered his father's principles. The way he dished up the basics around the dinner table. 'Don't get involved in the drugs,' he'd said, he'd been firm on that. His da even had some respect for the residents that had come out and picketed the dealers' houses, shamed criminals at their own front door. The big man felt a useless guilt about it, but what else was there now? You couldn't be a so-called Ordinary Decent Criminal any more. They were being squeezed out by the big drugs gangs the way chain stores were killing local businesses. He'd heard one of the old-timers say that.

In his da's day, early on, there had just been the pickpockets and burglars. It had been altogether sleepier, old fashioned. But they took it ahead a level, in the seventies, with the police caught up in the Troubles. They moved it up to armed robbery. All that aside, they resisted drugs. They knew it would come down in their back garden. The 'blaggers', there was something clean and romantic to that, doing over a bank. Something heroic somehow. His da got out after the Athy gang were taken down. That was a bloodbath. But he spoke about the scores with a kind of moral pride. 'It was us against the banks,' he used to say, 'us against the government.' Like some great big story, thought the big man. *Now we're all against each other. You don't know who you can trust. You just have to keep your head down. Stay out of the other guy's patch. Everything's changed now.*

'Da never would have lasted in it,' he thought. 'He had too much conscience. Those young blaggers that started with him became the grown-up drug barons. They moved things on as well,' he thought. 'It's natural. After those Dunnes flooded it all up with heroin, you couldn't turn that round. Things had changed. Then all this wealth came in. It kind of made a niche for me. There wasn't any of this killing work before the drugs.' He chewed the tuna paste sandwich. *Da would have understood that*; but he felt this guilt.

'It'll disease the community,' his father had said. The big man felt the useless guilt again. It was a different age, the way things had gone. 'Maybe it's lucky Da went before all of this,' he thought.

He watched the boy in the tracksuit disappear down the street, saw the traffic lights up ahead go

177

amber then green like some kind of Catholic parade. There was still this violence coming off Stringer.

He thought of the traffic lights and the colour of the flag and of his father's great pride in the place. 'He tried to get us out,' he thought. 'I always knew where I was with his lessons. And then with Mikey. But now I feel like a big crashed down tree floating around in the ocean. It's just too big out here. The world's too big.' He looked out at the overwhelming street. 'I'm floating in it and I have no idea what to do unless someone tells me.' He knew underneath he was an instrument. He knew ultimately he was one of those men to be wielded, not the arm behind those men.

'I had to do something, Da,' he said inside, 'and I never knew how to do anything else.' He'd kind of lost anchor when his brother had died and that's why he stuck to Stringer. 'I'm an instrument. A big, blunt instrument,' he thought. That wasn't so bad though. 'Like String says, I'm a natural.'

Hold pushed open the door and expected there to be the dull clang of a shop bell or something to announce him but there was nothing and he stood in the hallway with the bag of rabbits and looked at the information leaflets that were on a table and the thin corridor and the stairs right in front of him. There was a sign saying 'out by ten'. He felt the cold in the place and glanced down at his coat still over the coolbag to hide the rabbits. The hallway was the kind of place that never got the sun and it seemed to hold this coldness.

He went up the stairs. There was an egg smell from the café next door. The steps were carpeted and had the little metal arms for holding the carpet down at the edges just like in the old house. The stairs were loud with the hollowness of what he thought was a cwtch beneath them, and there were uneven pictures on the wall, the kind you could buy from a supermarket. Then, someone called to him below.

He stopped on the stairs and went down and there was a grey, pinched looking woman and he didn't know where she'd come from. She looked at him incuriously and nodded.

'*Oes 'stafell 'da chi?*'

'*Oes. Am faint?*' There was the nasal, North Walian sound.

'Just *henno.*'

She looked at the bag he was carrying and asked him if he had any other bags to go and get and he said he didn't and she nodded and gestured passively at the stairs.

The room was cheap and she asked him to pay up front and opened one of the rooms with a bunch of keys from her apron and put the money and the keys back in the apron.

'*Brecwast?*' he asked.

'*Drws nesa. Cun naw. Mas erbyn deg.*'

The woman nodded again and pointed passively at the key that was on the bed with an oversized fob.

'Leave it in the room when you go,' she said in English. It was like she wanted him to know it was clear he didn't speak Welsh all the time.

He went into the room and heard her go away. The carpet was worn in front of the door. The bed sagged.

He went into the bathroom. The bathroom was just a box with no window or ventilation and the toilet paper was all curled up at the two edges with the steam that had been in the place previously.

He used the toilet and it flushed weakly and he went back into the room and took the oversized fob off the key and put the key in his pocket.

He sat on the bed and it gave unconvincingly under him and he looked round the room. There was a deal table by the window and a tired chair and this thing that he didn't understand with a frame and straps of seatbelt material. There was a wardrobe and the kettle and tea were on the floor on a tray by a socket. There were big gaps around the bottom and top of the door like it had been planed down to fit and round the lock there were coverings of extra paint. He looked at the thing with the seatbelt straps. He put the rabbits on the floor by the bed and looked at them for a long time, then he looked out of the window.

He sat down on the chair. He looked at the strange metal bar over the head of the bed with its cushions hanging from it in place of a headboard.

He took out the phone. The noise of the homeward traffic came from down the street.

He looked at the embroidered scenes on the cushions that showed a stag hunt, the stag twisted and leaping.

'Maybe I should have brought the gun,' he thought.

Stringer seethed at the traffic. In the

last ten or fifteen years the city had exploded. The growth had been ferocious in this period they talked about as the Celtic Tiger. To Stringer, the city was like a child he used to play with who had suddenly grown up, that he didn't recognise any more. In the time he'd been inside, things had changed, as if it had done so while his back was turned, played a cheap kid's trick on him. He was waiting for the Tiger to turn round and bite them, hoped for it with this mean little glee.

The standard of living had gone up drastically, seeming to put this new coat of paint on the people in the city, but the cost of living had soared too. That opened it up for incomers, people who didn't understand the place, thought Stringer. People who were there to take from it. He'd read somewhere that it had got to be one of the richest cities in the world, and it was like the child he couldn't recognise any more going on to stardom, leaving him behind. Not wanting to recognise a dirty cousin would be closer to the truth, he thought. He couldn't stand other people's success. He cursed inside at the traffic, the shiny new cars with their EU number plates, the new mobility of the place. He could see from where they were, through the low buildings, the tall cone of the Spire. 'Look at that,' he thought. 'Look at that pointless thing. The tallest street sculpture in the world,' he thought with disgust. 'The stiletto in the ghetto.' He nearly spat that thought. One hundred and twenty metres of brushed steel. It always looked different, depending on the light, and unlike Stringer, it seemed to light up in dull conditions. He hated what it represented, this reaching for the skies of the new city. He felt angry at losing his sense of identity. 'Aren't we smart,' he thought. He felt the place had the sick broadcast of the reformed. 'It's not lasting though,' thought Stringer with this secret hope. 'I learnt some things inside.' He prided himself on his little intelligences. 'This won't last. It happened too quickly, there's nothing behind it. Like a bolted plant. The honey'll run out and it will collapse in.' He was proud of his intelligence about it. He thought about all the books he'd read inside. Reading was the only way to feel like you were moving in there. 'I have acumen,' he thought. He said that word in his mind again, savouring it. 'All that European money getting pumped in. It's like a big guy on steroids, the muscles won't work properly.' *Already the paint's flaking off.*

He'd been thinking. He'd been letting the petty jealousy of the warm little house fester in him. 'It's okay for him,' he thought, 'that big overgrown bastard. His da got them out.' He could smell the tuna paste sandwiches. 'Putting a kid in those places, that's like putting horseshit round a plant. It makes them grow. If I'd have had that, I'd have made more of myself instead of always having to scrap around. I've got brains,' he thought.

He thought back to Blessington Street, the way they were weeded out of the slums into the corporation housing, the hideous blocks and boarded-up lower storeys of Dominick Street. He thought of the stints as a kid in the industrial schools, the horror of the Brothers. He looked at the big man in the front seat eating through the sandwiches. 'How has he never been inside?' he thought. He looked at him like he was some big, passive forty-year-old child and he was disgusted by him.

'I got overlooked. I should have been up for one of the big strokes.'

He stared furiously out of the window at the immobile traffic.

'There's the explosion,' thought Stringer, 'and then

183

there's the in-suck as things collapse in the vacuum, the lack of anything these booms can make.' Stringer congratulated himself on this little speech he'd just made. 'Either way, it suits us. Bring in the money, and the cocaine market thrives, the disposable income goes where people want to dispose of it. Bring things down, and you got disillusion, heroin, people taking their escapes any way they could. They were wrong, those old guys, not to get involved. It's sure-fire, this business,' thought Stringer. 'It's a business now, that's why I studied things inside. I thought I'd get my chance at a crew. I've got brains.'

Stringer thought bitterly of the others, all up there now while he'd done his time, the stretch in the Joy, in Portlaoise.

'Seven years,' he thought. 'Seven years of emptying out my own piss-pot every morning.'

'I put it in,' he felt. 'I deserve a shot at a big stroke.' It's all politics now, he thought bitterly again. He could hear the driver and the big man talking about hurling teams but was in a world of his own. 'He deserved it,' he told himself. 'That culchie. He shouldn't have pushed me. I couldn't just ignore it.' He was looking at the flaky skin on the driver's shoulders. He seemed to focus on it slowly.

'Seven years' head start they got on me. And they don't have my brains. I deserve a chance to make something of myself.'

They hadn't moved for ten minutes or so and then

184

they heard the sirens and the half-still cars seemed to peel to the sides of the road like an opening zip and the ambulance went past them dangerously fast.

The crash had happened further on, out of sight, and the traffic had solidified. It brought Stringer back round. He hated to stay still. He was like a shark, something that had to keep moving. The germ of a little idea was getting hold of Stringer and he was letting it, as if he was happy watching it grow. 'It's just about getting myself some start.'

'We'll have to take the DART,' he said.

The two men got out of the car and started to head to the station on foot through the stilled traffic. Stringer was walking quickly and funnily like he wouldn't wait for the big man, like a parent fed up of a kid dawdling in a shopping street. The big man trotted behind. He'd left the rest of the sandwiches in the car as some kind of apology.

The red-faced man watched them go and absently scratched his eczema. 'That Stringer's a prick,' he muttered, through one of the big man's sandwiches.

Hold went out to get some food.

He left the rabbits in the bag in the room. I have to eat, he told himself. It's just basic discipline. He had to still think, force himself to stay sharp. With the waiting there were no tests and he knew he had to put them upon himself, to keep sharp.

As he swallowed the mug of stale coffee he thought hard about just going. He knew that he had in some way left the rabbits in the room so that he could. So that he could simply get in the van and drive away now. He imagined the woman finding the bag in the wardrobe and cursing, and assuming he'd forgotten them. There was nothing to connect him. The key would be gone, but that would be just another lock change, if she bothered. He banked she'd throw the rabbits. He imagined the high, dismembered carcasses rotting down on some council dump. The crows picking over them and the forty thousand pound packages falling from the split middles.

'Eat, you have to eat,' he told himself. 'Don't think like this. You know you're doing this so don't get distracted. Don't take your eyes off it. Get some food.'

He finished the coffee and went over to the Spar and bought a hot pasty. He stood outside the shop looking down the street to the rooming house, half expecting to see someone come from it with the bag.

He turned round and read the window cards and saw an advert for a car for two hundred pounds. It seemed to unlock an idea that was already in him. He read the card again then he took down the number. He went down the street between the stallholders, who were dismantling the market now, and found a cash point. Two hundred quid. It was pretty much everything he had. If it can get me out of this, that's what it'll take.

'It'll do me well,' he thought, 'to have another car. If anything goes wrong they can't trace me that way. They can't get back to Cara and Jake. They'd have people in the police. There are bent people everywhere. I can't leave an obvious link back to them.' He thought of being stopped earlier, of the documents in the box again. 'I don't want them to be able to trace me.'

He was close to a fish van and they were packing up for the day and he got the smell of the tired fish and thought of the bait pots and was suddenly in his mind back on the boat. He had a brief longing for that freedom.

He took the money and went to a phone box.

The two men were outside a bar

and looked out over the port and at the big waiting ferry. There was a chill breeze.

'What's that smell?' asked the big man. He screwed up his big face a bit, like he was squinting, like he couldn't sniff properly.

'That's the sea,' said Stringer. 'I'm surprised you can smell anything with those things.'

The big man smoked and Stringer bullied him

about it. There was a chill to the air of the port and the big man was trying to light the big gas patio heater.

The ticking of the lighter was going over and over. There was something unpredictable about the smaller man. He was sitting there all compacted in his long coat.

'Give it up,' he said. The big man didn't know whether he was talking about the smoking or trying to light the heater but he stopped trying to light the heater and just smoked.

Stringer was bald and small and criminal looking. He was like a rat. They could see the cars queuing up to go onto the ferry.

'What you want to smoke for? It's freezing right now.' There were the clanks and echoes of the port.

'I won't be able to smoke on the boat.'

'You can go outside to smoke on the boat.'

'I've never been over before.'

Stringer looked at him with this kind of quiet disbelief.

'Well, you can smoke on the boat.'

Stringer looked out over the port. He thought back to the strokes, to the stroke that had put him inside, properly inside, for the first time. It didn't happen here, but the wet salt smell in the air and the round metallic sounds of loading were the same as the docks.

It was simple. They had bogus documentation, fitted the trucks with false plates and just drove in and hooked up to the containers. Then they just drove out. Rossi had connections, of course, on the docks, but it was an easy stroke.

Rossi wouldn't like what's happened, thought Stringer. The drugs. He was always against them. His neighbours down on Pearse Street saw him as some kind of guardian, this necessary evil, like some Robin Hood. He kept the dealers out. Everybody feared him.

Stringer wanted to be feared. He wanted to be powerful. He sat there with his little clock of fury ticking away. 'I went down for one of his strokes,' he said to himself. 'I never said a word. I deserve more than I got.'

He looked at the big man smoking. 'You big overgrown bastard,' he thought.

'Maybe we shouldn't have got here so early,' thought Stringer. He could feel his energies festering in him.

He thought back to that first stretch. Somehow the thoughts of the industrial schools and the borstals were dormant in his mind, as if he had removed the animation from them. Those were factual things of his past and seemed to be all one thing that sat distastefully in his head like a stuffed family pet in a cabinet. But the Joy was different. That seven years. The way the culchie's face had started to come open.

He looked out over the port, cold, cursing inside at the necessity for the big man. 'I liked that cold, when

189

I first got out,' he remembered to himself. 'No one tells you that. You expect to miss the rides, beer, a proper bed. A bathroom to yourself. But no one can tell you the other things. When you come out after a long time you're like a kid for weeks with everything. Cold air, natural cold air like this. Opening a fridge door.

'Freedom is a funny thing,' thought Stringer. 'We're all in prison, some way or another. Just you don't see it.' He thought of the books he'd read. 'There's four walls round all of us, and some screw who pushes a tray through your door. That's it. Even the top guys have got it that way.'

He looked out and watched as a guy walked past the pub wall with his wife, two kids and a dog. 'That's four walls right there,' said Stringer to himself. 'A wife, two kids and a dog. That's enough to keep you in it.'

The big man was trying with the lighter again, the patio heater clicking and clicking.

'Give that up, will you,' Stringer said. The big man gave up. He looked at Stringer forlornly. At the port, they were starting to roll the trucks on to the ferry and there were low, booming echoes going round. By now, the big man was losing his sense of excitement and was mildly nervous of the sea. He was nervous of Stringer too. He could be unpredictable. What could you do? He'd been good to his brother. Family was important to the big man.

Stringer watched the family with the dog head

190

down the steps to the port.

'We're all in it,' thought Stringer. 'Even the guys at the top.'

The man closed the bag.

'How is he?' asked the Scouser.

The man made a non-committal face. 'You never know with him,' he said. The bag sat heavily on his lap. 'I think he's enjoying the sun out there.'

'Thank him. For the opportunity,' said the Scouser. If you wanted to operate here, you had to buy the right. You could try to just muscle your way in but the business way was better. There was a hierarchy. Respect was important, he understood that.

'Just keep making the money.' The man made the non-committal face again. 'Is there anything you need?'

'No,' said the Scouser. 'We've had a few problems, a few missing packets, but we're handling it.'

'You can't let that get out of hand,' said the man.

He felt the needles. He let them go through his body deliciously and thought of the Irishmen, soon to be on the water. There was kind of a fine meanness to him.

The man was looking at him.

'No,' said the Scouser. 'It's under control.'

Hold called up the number and asked about the car and the woman called to her son and the son said it was still up for sale. He said it didn't have the MOT for much longer, and could probably do with new tyres and Hold said it didn't matter about the MOT and the tyres. Hold took down the directions the boy gave him.

He went down onto the main road that ran parallel with the inner harbour and walked along until he came to the taxi place he'd noted earlier. It was grubby looking. The sort of place you'd associate with much bigger towns.

He went in and asked for a car and one of the guys inside got up from one of the chairs. A few of them were watching a television set mounted up in the corner like in a takeaway.

They went outside and Hold got into the taxi and the driver repeated the name of the place and Hold gave him the directions again. He didn't want to talk. He could feel the roll of money in his pocket. That was the last of it. It'll get me through, he thought. The driver had an air freshener plugged into the lighter socket and it stank out the car and he turned on the radio just low enough for Hold not to hear.

'Suits me,' said Hold. He didn't want to talk. It was like he had lost the habit of discussion in this strange singular place he'd come to. It felt like longer. 'It's just two days,' thought Hold. *The old life was way gone.*

They drove out of the town past the thick train lines and over the bridge and peeled right off a roundabout through continuous estates of houses. To the sides of them in the evening light the fields showed flatly between the settlements and the dipping sun spread in the grease of the window so it was like looking through a thin, painful cloth.

They came into another estate of houses and Hold counted off the turnings until they reached the place. 'This is it,' Hold said.

He paid the driver and the car went away and Hold walked past the red Fiesta in the driveway and up to the door. The boy came out and they went over the car. The documents were in the dash.

'Will you take one seventy-five?' Hold asked the boy. He made a show of looking at the tyres and kicked them absently.

'That's fine,' said the boy.

By the time Hold started back, the sun had gone down.

Hold drove the car into town and

took out the documents and put them into a bin and went over the car again. Then he went back to the room and plugged the phone in to charge and lay back on the bed, below the stag scenes, listening to the sporadic traffic. He thought of the dead Pole. The words in his head. *Checkham.*

He got up and took two of the big anti-inflammatories and went over things in his mind. 'You've thought of it. You just have to wait. You've thought of everything now. You just have to wait for the call. It will come.' He took the bag out from the wardrobe and sat there, just looking at the rabbits and waiting.

The phone rang just after nine o'clock. Hold didn't say anything, he just picked it up. He was sitting on the bed looking out through the window. For a while the other man didn't say anything either. Hold looked across at the glow coming off a kebab shop sign across the road. Then the man spoke.

'It'll happen tomorrow afternoon.'

'Where?'

'We'll tell you where.' Hold could feel the voice lick out at him, taste him. Hold was focusing in on the pause, trying to discern anything he could. It was like watching for movement.

'We'll have your money. Ten thousand minus the cost of the boat we lost. You'll get seven thousand.'

Hold's head spun. He waited, trying to sound flat but there were waves of adrenaline in him.

'Ten?' The blood pounded his ears.

'Seven. You lost the boat.'

Hold tried to hold the spin down, the glow from the kebab shop seemed like it was dropped in water, blurring. 'Come on, come on,' he was saying to himself. The 'seven thousand' kept sounding over and over into his head. He saw in his mind the clear picture of the dead Pole and the phone in the boat. For *ten* thousand.

'I know how much these packets are worth,' he tried.

'Find another buyer then.'

'Maybe I'll come and get the money myself,' said Hold. For a moment he'd lost focus, was dangerously thrown. He had no idea what he was doing. He tried to put this convincing threat in his voice to unnerve the other man.

'What do you think this is?' There was a horrible, tangible calm violence. 'Who do you think you're dealing with here? You think we're amateurs?'

The man's nerve held. He was rhythmic, calm.

'They're worth a lot more,' said Hold.

'*They* are. But the job isn't. That's how it works.' The voice paused. 'You think the guy that delivers leather sofas charges the cost of the sofa?' The voice paused again. It was almost gentle, didactic. A tired giving out of knowledge. Hold could feel the miscalculation, the short-sightedness sink into him.

'It's worth ten thousand, minus the boat you lost.' Again, the voice was giving Hold time to fill up with the cold facts of it. 'And the life of the other guy's family.' That was the final little trap.

Hold felt a blip of anger. Of sheer dizzying comprehension.

'If you do anything to—'

'What?' The voice railed finally. 'What? You'll come for me? Grow up. You might get past one guy. You might kill the next flunky along. You think you'll get to me?'

The voice went quiet again.

'It's nothing to do with them.'

'Make sure it isn't.' The phone stayed quiet. Then it went dead.

Hold just sat there with his head in his hands and couldn't think.

The two men walked past the gardaí

onto the ferry over the gangplank and handed over their landing cards and went into the boat. The passengers inside were spreading out to explore the levels of the boat. It was stuffy inside and smelled like someone was trying to cover up some other smell. There wasn't any moving air in it. Already you could hear the thrum of the huge engines and the noise of the vehicles loading on downstairs.

The two men went up to the top lounge and took seats and looked over the port and out to the sea. There was a chop coming to it and the little white crests showed up in the light that spilled out into the bay from the port now in the dark. The big man was sure the ferry was the wrong way round to start the journey.

Out on the dock a JCB worked in floodlight moving stone, picking through the boulders like it had intelligence, and the dust of the moved stones whirled in the light like moths about him. The way the machine looked deft was like the big man making a cigarette. The lounge smelled of stale pubs and the chairs swivelled and tilted back and forth. There were big No Smoking signs everywhere inside.

Stringer got up without saying anything and went down a deck to the bureau de change and got some pounds and came back and gave some to the big man. The bar was filling up with people and some of the people were drinking already, and some were looking over the snack menu. There were children running about like in a park. The lounge was really high off the water.

When they were under way Stringer went off to the gambling area and in a while came back and said, 'Let's go eat.'

They went down to the restaurant level and ate. The restaurant was like a service station restaurant.

From the middle of the restaurant where they sat you couldn't see anything but the dark sky and its oddness in the lights of the ferry. The windows were all scratched with salt like there was a glaucoma to them.

They were coming out and gathering, like birds dropping in to roost at dusk, starting to line the end of the street. He slowed the car down. He had a plan, and he'd kind of snatched at it. He had no idea how this went. He slowed the car right down and pulled in to the curb and after a moment a girl walked over. She stood while he wound down the passenger window and leant in and asked him if he was looking for business. She wore a short skirt and a puffer jacket. He looked at the black puffer jacket like the Pole had worn. He noticed when she leant in how lank the hair looked.

'Any foreign girls?' he asked. The puffer jacket had prompted this quick thought. He looked in the mirror. Behind him the girls were writing down his number and the time in their notebooks. There were about six girls now. They were smoking and chewing gum and looked cold. There was none of the American glamour to it.

'Ani!' the girl called over and walked away.

The girl called Ani walked over. A. Another A he thought. It was like a strange sign. She was pale and

198

underfed and when she leant in he saw the cheekbones
and he said:

'Where are you from?'

And she said 'Europe.'

He said, 'Get in,' and she opened the door and
looked him up and down and then she made some
signal to the other girls and got in and shut the door.

'*Checkham*,' he said. 'What does it mean?'

She looked at him.

'Is it a name? *Checkham. Vrooj prosser checkham*?'

'I don't know.' Her accent was thick.

'Is it the way I'm saying it?'

'I don't know what you're saying,' she said.

She looked round onto the back seat, at the
coolbag with the rabbits, and he saw on her bare legs
the roughened red skin of the knees and the bruises at
the tops of her thighs disappearing under the skirt. He
didn't feel anything for her.

'What do you want to do?' she said prettily.
'You're good looking.' She was wearing a denim jacket
and she took it off and he could see the small red bra
through her shirt and the points of her breasts pushed
forward as she leaned to get the jacket off in the seat.

'Who runs you?' he said.

'What?'

'Who runs you? Who runs the girls?' She began to
get scared.

'Don't get out of the car,' he said. He said it really

factually and she sat back.

'Who are you?' she asked. 'Are you police?' She said police like two little words.

'No, I'm not police.' He held up some of the money in his hands. 'Put the jacket back on,' he said. He could see the goosebumps on her arms.

He gave her a twenty.

'Who runs you?' he asked. He looked dead at her. Her face was like the woman from the phone photos. Colder, hungrier, younger, but like her. The structure was the same.

'I don't understand,' she said.

'Who is in charge of you? Who is the boss?'

'We look after each other. Girls,' she said. It was cold in the car. 'I don't understand.'

Hold waited, looked at her.

'Where can I buy drugs around here? Cocaine?' The other girls were now looking at the car that hadn't moved. He gave her more money.

'No drugs,' she said. 'Clean.' He could feel that her nerves were up. The other girls were coming up to the car.

'Where are you from?' he asked.

'Europe.'

'Where?' He was looking at the bone structure. The wide apart eyes.

'Europe,' she said.

She grabbed the jacket and got out of the car and

left the door open like it was practised. She was holding the money.

'Bastard,' she shouted. The girl who had come over first was on the phone. He turned on the engine. '*Checkham*,' he said. 'What is it? Is it a name?'

He was looking her right in the eye. '*Vrooj prosser checkham.*' He felt the car nod and heard the crackle as one of the girls put her heel through the rear light, and then he drove off.

At eleven o'clock, the ferry was about half way through its crossing.

The big man was out on the promenade deck. He just wanted to lie down but could not. He was staring down at the pools the rain had left as they sloshed back and forth at the bulkheads. Nothing he had tried had made him feel better but he had stopped being sick.

'This is a bad sign,' he thought. 'I should never have left Dublin. Water's not good luck for us.'

He looked down at the luminous waves, cresting in the unusual light. He'd been sick into his hand on the way out of the restaurant and had thrown it into a urinal and gone and thrown up over and over, all this half-chewed peas and fish and the paste of half-digested sandwiches coming out of him. The pile of it sat and stank in the urinal, and when it flushed automatically it washed the mess out onto the floor. It was peagreen and mixed with the piss where people had missed. The big man felt like death. He looked like he was at prayer over the urinal and in the way he felt it was possible he was.

Stringer came out from the gambling room and found the big man and saw that he had got the shakes. Stringer blasphemed at him.

The big man couldn't get the stink of sick out of his hands. He hadn't brought a toothbrush, nothing to wash with, and he felt a strange embarrassment at the idea of buying a toothbrush, a vulnerableness in society. Things that had always been done for him by his mother. He welcomed the cold, trying to numb himself.

'Jesus, have a fucking cigarette,' said Stringer.

'I can't smoke,' said the big man.

The slow ferry loped on, with its puking and petting and playing passengers, regardless of them all, through a sea that was getting up, a sea that had, it seemed, some sense of duty, a vital job, as if, should it stop, the world would stop. For a while there had been a brief squall of rain but it had no feeling to the ferry at all. It just plodded on towards the port where the other man was waiting, taking the two men towards him.

He took the rabbits and the money

and everything else he had in the car and left the car parked up just off the bridge. Then he tucked himself into an alley between the big wheelie bins. He threw the keys into the bin.

Initially he'd got the car to make the handover in, just so they couldn't trace him back after. He was sure the gang would have connections with the police. He'd even felt a small guilt considering they might work back to the boy and the mother he'd got the car off, but this was an outside chance he told himself. They'd work it out, surely.

It was only when the call had come, the bombshell of the seven thousand, that he'd thought of trying to sell the drugs himself. The plan was deranged from the start and not thought out, he saw that now. To try and get to some local drug pusher by assuming the girls would be involved. It's not a film. It's not a god-damned film he told himself. Asking for the foreign girl had been a spur of the moment thing.

In a while a car came along and stopped, and reversed back to the Fiesta with the broken rear light. Two guys got out. They looked over the car. Then they worked it over with baseball bats and drove off.

'I guess that's it,' said Hold to himself. 'I see it through now. That was just an idea. It was just a nervous mistake, thinking I could get the drugs moved on another way. The best is if I just see it through now.'

After a while he came out from the alley and walked a little way and went up the pedestrianised area and to the church and rested on the old wall and looked at the rabbits. Seven thousand. That was the way it was going to be. He studied the herringbone pattern of the stones. He just wanted it over now.

He thought of the wide face of the girl. He thought of the Pole making his ten thousand pound shot. 'Ten thousand isn't enough. It's nothing,' he thought. 'Seven thousand. It won't change anything. Not one time only.'

He worked out in his head that if his story about the fish had been true, he could have got close to a thousand. Somehow that figure seemed more real. 'Maybe I could get my own boat with seven thousand,' he was thinking. 'Try and work something out about the house with Danny's sister.'

The huge ferry had just come in and the cars started to come past him on the road just below and filter out, most of them heading south off the island. The noises of the unloading boomed comfortably round the dock. The ferry was truly immense. Watching the cars come out and spread lithely away, Hold thought of the mouth-brooding fish who keep their young safe in their mouths when there's danger. He felt some sense of safety, of comfort in the decision just to finish this. He could put the money away for the boy, or take some to go game fishing with in

204

Florida. Imagine that. *Imagine a big marlin coming out of the water. That would be something, just once in your life. To see something like that, magnificent in its own element – I couldn't kill it though. Maybe I couldn't even fish it. What would it be for, really? It would just be to see it, and I don't know if there's any other way to see it than to fish it.*

The big floodlights lit up the ship like a cathedral. He watched the cars unload for a long time, saw the huge boat lift in the water as it gradually shed its load. Tired as he was, there was something mesmeric about it.

The two men came off the ferry.

It looked odd, Stringer helping the huge big man down the gangway, as if he was some kind of handler of a big dangerous animal made drowsy with something.

Around the boat, the foot passengers spread out across the quay. The priest-like man helped the big man along, and amongst the crowd of the tired and drunk and of the people confused by the strange process of travel they were simply another exhibit.

The priest-like figure left the big man afloat on the wide tarmac of the disembarkation area for a while and went over to a taxi driver who was parked among a flock of cars that looked bizarre and luminous under the spilling bright floodlights.

They talked briefly, and then Stringer went over and collected the suffering big man and got him in the taxi, and the three characters headed off away from the port.

From the taxi, Stringer saw a guy leant up on the wall staring out over the still emptying ferry. He looked odd up there, alone, somehow painted on against the floodlights that lit up the church behind.

The bag next to the man on the wall seemed to give out some light of its own in the residual floodlight from the church, some beckoning statement.

It was kind of mesmeric and eyedrawing in the strangeness of it.

'I'm tired,' thought Stringer. He was tired on many levels.

They drove on under the wall, and the man glanced down only briefly as the taxi went past and went away out of sight.

The big man was in the front seat. He was still ill.

Stringer spoke. 'Drive around a bit,' he said in his nervous Irish voice to the owlish man at the wheel. 'I want to see where to do this.'

Part Four

The two men sat in a caff. Both men wore gloves. They were thin leather gloves and they looked somehow feminine on the big man.

It was early and grey fog came in from the port and messed the light about. It was dismal. The big man still looked rough as hell. They sat in the back of the caff and could smell the kitchen through the door.

The man had met them as arranged. It was disorientating to come off the boat at that time of night. The man, done up like a regular taxi driver, had given them the black sports bag and the bag was now under the table by Stringer's feet. He was looking at the menu card. Up by the windows there were a few men sitting at tables on their own eating. They looked like lorry drivers. It was a fairly plastic place.

The waitress came up and asked them what they wanted. She was not pretty but she had a big chest.

Stringer had a thing for that, as if he missed his mother. It was difficult to see how it would work with him being so small as he was.

The girl with the big chest came over and put some toast down on the table and asked what they wanted.

'What's a full Welsh?' asked Stringer.

'It's like a full English,' said the girl.

'Okay. I'll have a full Welsh.'

The girl went away. The big man had just shaken his head. The girl thought that maybe the gloves were because they were queers or something.

'You should eat,' Stringer said. He took a piece of toast and started to spread it still with his gloves on. The toast was so cold the butter didn't melt on it. The big man looked horrific.

'Some scary bastard you are,' Stringer said. The big man looked at Stringer then and something went through Stringer and he couldn't have said what it was. It made him look down at the bag under the table then away at the men at the other tables but it was like the big man's eyes had been horribly left in him. Like they were rolling about inside him as he held the toast. That hadn't happened to Stringer before with anyone.

'Eat breakfast, you scary fuck!' he said.

Hold got up and gathered up the bag of rabbits and left the key on the bed and went out. He had not slept.

He went out onto the street. The thick mist sat in the street and he could see the minute drops shift in front of him with this great individuality. He was tired from not sleeping and spaced somehow and felt in some ways a great and dangerous carelessness now.

He went up out of the street to the van and got in and then turned on the engine and headed out of the town slowly in the fog.

'There's a way out,' he said. 'I don't need the money. It's not worth the risk. And I don't want these any more, it's like they've become some part of me.' It was as if the drugs had some voice to him now, as if they had taken on a little song.

He drove out of the town with this numb decisive sense and headed into the island and it was as if the fog thickened and the further he got the less he could see.

'It's closing around me,' he thought.

'And you're sure it's clear?' said Stringer. He thought of the big man getting to the boat.

'It's better in the day,' said the owlish man. 'Kids in school. People in work. And we should use this.' The owlish man gestured at the fog.

'What about the water?' The man from the city did not know about the tides so well.

'It shouldn't be enough to move the body much. But you'll have to make sure the stuff stays with him.'

That had been the Scouser's call. Leave the link there. Make it clear the thing was drug related, send a little ripple out...

'We'll make sure,' said Stringer. But there was this growing germ in him.

The big man waded through the knee-deep water. He could feel the slight tug of the water as the tide went out. The fog licked around him, and every half a minute or so came the far off sound of the foghorn from the Stack. It was like some slow pulse, some clock.

He swung the bag into the boat and climbed himself with the surprising agility he had up the thin aluminium ladder at the back and got out of the water and uncertainly in. As soon as his legs were out of the water he could feel the cold on them. He sat on the side of the boat looking much too big for it and the boat shifted strangely under him, half afloat in the shallow water. He took off his shoes and emptied out the water over the side of the boat. Then he peeled off his socks and wrung them out over the side into the ebbing water. He looked down at the bag as if checking it was safe.

The fog came round him and the boats in the line around seemed to peer oddly at the big man sitting there unsteadily on the boat. They appeared like half-coloured shapes through an opaque window. He could feel the boat lull and bounce unexpectedly with the water and hunkered, as if his big weight could keep the boat still. Already the memory of the sick came to him like a taste.

'It's always me,' thought the big man to himself. He could feel the cold getting into the bones of his feet. His toes looked strange to him, bleached and drained of blood in the water.

He looked at the way the boats in-line appeared oddly through the fog and remembered the guy in the sauna at the massage parlour, the way his face seemed to form out of the thin steam when he'd gone in to get him, the scorched meaty smell of his face on the coals, the force he'd had to use to get him off the coals afterwards like it was an egg stuck to a pan.

'There's always something,' he thought. 'Always some little thing to put up with.' The foghorn came again, repetitively. It could grate on you. He remembered the irritation of the sweat pouring into his eyes as he did the sauna job. 'This time it's just cold. And these damn boats,' he thought. 'There's always something.'

He looked back down at his feet. 'They look like a dead man's feet,' he thought. 'They look like Mikey's feet when they pulled him out of the Liffey.' He reached for his socks and put the wet socks on again to cover up his feet, thinking of his dead brother. Then he put his shoes on, and got down in the belly of the boat.

Hold pulled the van up in the shallow gateway at the side of the road. He took the knife and slit open the rabbits, nicking the nylon stitches that had bitten into the hardening flaps of skin and were sunk down hidden in the fur. The icepacks had long since lost the ice and the inside of the bag had gone warm and the smell was starting to come off the rabbits. The condensation from the temperature changing in the bag had stuck their fur in clumps and they looked bedraggled and undignified now, like wet leaves.

It was very early and the first light was stretching out and amplified by the fog and it was white and directionless. Every thirty seconds or so, Hold could hear the low moan of the lighthouse foghorn, but it was faint, almost imperceptible.

Then there on the side of the road, Hold wet some toilet paper he had taken from the room and wiped off the blood that had dried chocolate red on the packages and put the three packages in a carrier bag.

He looked out over the field disappearing into the fog with the light coming up and thought back. He thought back to the similarly short rabbit-cropped grass of the slopes above the cliffs, of the gull-dropped shells and desiccated mermaid's purses, the broken bits of crab that scattered about in the short grass, bleaching in the salt and light. He thought of the slow uncoiling of the rabbits when they were shot, this kind of easement of the tension something hunted must live under and he felt the bedraggled dampened carcasses there in his hands.

Maybe it can be the same, he thought. This money won't change anything, it's not enough. It is only I that know about this, and if I can close that away somewhere so no one else can see it, then there's no reason why things can't just be the same.

He thought back over the long distance of the last day.

No one is affected by this, nothing changes, he thought. I can just go back to how it was. I was right. I was right not to bring the gun.

He sat in the van for a while, not focusing anywhere. He was back on the boat, running the knife through the fillets, feeling the minute bump of the knife break through the glaceous rib bones with this train track rhythm.

He noted the foghorn again and somewhere an oystercatcher called, startled. He could feel himself gathering, coming together. Just one thing to think of, then he could return to it all. There would be other ways to sort the problems, or other things that grew from whatever happened in the wake of them. But there would always be the beach, the long nets, the company of the tides. 'You can't rescue everyone,' he thought. 'People survive their own way.' He felt the gathering, the coming together. 'I was right not to bring the gun.' He looked down at the rabbits prone there in his hands.

'One last thing,' he said. 'One more thing. This is the last part.'

Then he threw the empty rabbits into the field.

After a while the call of the foghorn

got to the big man as he lay in the boat and he had started to wait for the sound like the tick of some slowed-down clock, like a drip of tap water. It was a small torture. The tide had gone out. He could feel the boat bump and settle under him, and even though the lurches were brief and small they had been tiring and made him nervy, every time thinking the boat would go over. He was cold and sick feeling and could feel the insipid fog seep into him. 'This is the last time with the boats,' he thought. 'I feel like I've been in it for hours.'

He remembered getting on the DART, Stringer losing his temper with the ticket machine. The big man had always liked trains, whatever sort. He'd felt calm on it, not like the damned boat. There was something he liked perhaps about the fact that a train could only go along the track that was put down for it, and you knew where that went from the start.

They went out of the stop and out along the line past the waterfront, the long wide stretch of water spanning out to the horizon, a strange mobile emptiness seeming to have this serene sense of success to it against the aspiration of the town. He'd felt somehow child-like going on this trip, though he knew, looking out over the water, of the unusual brutal purpose behind it.

'I've never been out of Ireland before,' he'd thought to himself. Stringer was looking up at the line map, counting off the stops, but it was hours until the ferry.

'I've hardly been out of the city,' he'd thought. He'd looked at the water and thought of his brother. 'He was different,' he thought. 'He had ambition. He tried to get out. I never had that.'

The big man had this crushing knowledge of what he was. And he couldn't do anything about it. He felt the useless guilt. 'Things changed,' he said to himself. 'I just followed you in, Da, but things had changed.'

He could still taste the tuna from the sandwiches, and kept finding little gouts of bread and fish cemented up in his teeth.

He'd sat there, riding the DART, happy looking for bits of sandwich with his tongue.

Hold stopped the van and took

the bag and got out and tasted immediately the sea in the rolling thick fog and followed the wooden arrowpost that marked the way up the mountain.

'There's a way,' he told himself.

He went slowly and blindly through the fog and here and there in patches it broke to give a sense of the surrounding ground, but then it souped again, and thickened.

He went slowly up the rising ground and halted at the outcrops of rock and at the busted gorse roots and at anywhere he thought might be secure and in the future locatable and then he stopped and just held the bag uselessly and realised the uselessness of the idea, that there was only one way to close this.

And the life of the other guy's family. The words stuck in his mind, seeped into him as if they came from the fog.

He stood for a long time, then he went back to finish things.

The big man felt too big for the space in the boat.

'What if I don't know when to go?' he thought. 'I can't look up from here. I have to do all this with my ears. There's always something... I have to get together though. Get ready now.'

From somewhere the smell of old fish came to him. It brought back the ferry ride. He hadn't eaten anything for hours and had been sick and his body was confused at the emptiness and at the same time the sickness at the thought of food. He could feel the aches setting in where his big body pressed up against the insides of the boat.

He thought of his brother. Boom. The maudlin call of the foghorn came again. 'He'd have fitted better in the boat,' thought the big man. He was more like Stringer, smaller and wiry. He partly put up with Stringer because of the likeness.

He thought of his brother's body being hauled out of the water, the strange bloated whiteness of the corpse, the odd feet. He tensed as he waited for the foghorn to sound, as if his body had fallen reluctantly in line with its rhythm. It was like being driven slowly mad. 'It's always me,' he thought. Then he heard the little chorus again, felt this friendly little knowledge. 'I'm better at it, I guess.' He felt a comfort going into it, reducing himself once more to an instrument. 'Think now, and be ready. Like Stringer says, I'm a natural.'

Hold pressed send. For what it was worth.

He did not abandon you. He tried to help. He tried to change it all for you. Do not hate him.

It was as if he could feel the text message dissipate

out into the sky around him, like some great religious thing somehow. Like it rolled out and out across the island and out over the channel to the mountains, rolling and rolling. And then the phone rang.

Hold pressed down the Jiffy bag

and wrote down the address on the front. He wondered briefly about writing something, some explanation but he could not, and then he just took the boy's knife which he had wrapped in tissue and dropped it into the Jiffy bag.

He held the envelope for a while. 'There'll be the postmark. If something happens. If something happens and... There will be the postmark.

'I can't write anything. If I write something there will be a finalism to it. If I don't write, I can just say I didn't want to take the knife into town. That they were checking vehicles going in. It's believable. I can go back from that. But if I write something...'

Then he dropped the Jiffy bag into the post.

'She'll understand,' he said. Inside he said that. 'She'll read it.'

The fog had kind of solidified into a

slow, thick rain that came sideways off the sea. The

man was standing on his own and Hold watched him from a distance. He couldn't see anyone else. As soon as he knew where it was to happen, he'd posted the knife and then got to the small beach and waited and watched the man come onto the beach by himself. The call had come and they had told him where to be and he had lied and said he was further away than he was, to give himself some time. 'I want somewhere more public,' he'd asked. It was still early, the fog discouraging, no one else about.

'You have an hour,' the Irishman had said.

He'd got there immediately, watched. Waited, and seen the man arrive. No one else.

Hold looked away from the binoculars and studied everything he could. He could feel inside him the physical sensing that he had had on the cliffs with the gun. A heightened sense. He looked into the few cars parked along the road and looked down at the small scab that was drying over the sore on his thumb. All the cars were empty.

'Why would they?' he was saying. 'Why would they do anything?' He could see the man getting impatient in the rain and he put the glasses down. He kept telling himself: it's worth forty thousand to them. Why would they do anything? Just think of the one thing now.

He brought the binoculars down. He could see the faint powdery white rimes on the grips that the salt had left from using them on the boat, remembered the view of the cliffs from the sea. On the dashboard, the beetle reappeared.

'I meant to put you out,' said Hold silently to it.

The beetle seemed to listen, gave the illusion of it, tasting the air. 'I'll do it when I get back,' he thought. It was like he was setting a superstitious trick for himself. 'I'll do it when I come back.'

He thought of Cara and Jake and he thought of his box of things tucked on the shelf amongst the tins in Danny's shed. He thought of the caravan and of rebuilding the house and he thought of the woman's voice on the phone and of the text message spreading out in the sky to her and of the thin undernourished prostitute and of the dead man. And then he made himself the way he was in the moments after he had pulled a trigger and he said, 'Okay, let's do this.'

He came up from the low part of the little dock and looked down at the sand for signs of anything. Any footprints, any signals. Anyone who might have gone on further than the man waiting there in the rain. There was nothing. The shore was lined with some of the first boats back into the water and they sat on the sand in the low tide. Along the line of seaweed there were the desiccated shells of sea potatoes, most of them broken.

The two men came together until they stood in the slow thick rain. Hold looked at the man. 'Well, if it's coming, it's coming now,' he thought.

'I guess that would be it.' The small man nodded at the bag. Hold nodded. He held it up and the rain made snapping noises on the carrier bag and then he slung it to the man a few feet from him.

The man's hand came out of his pockets for the first time and Hold noticed the black gloves and the man bent down watchfully and looked into the carrier bag. He wrapped up the bag and put it under his arm and stood up.

'Now it might come,' thought Hold.

The man unbuttoned his coat a way and reached in and took out a Jiffy bag and threw it to Hold.

'Seven thousand,' said the man.

The man waited a moment. 'You can count it if you want, but it's raining.'

He turned round and started walking off.

'That's it?' called Hold.

'That's it,' said the man over his shoulder.

Hold could feel the Jiffy bag give slightly and then the hard pad inside. It was as if, as the man walked off, he could hear the call of the packages receding. As if it was the sound of some transport going off into the distance.

It was dizzying almost, a vertigo, the relief and the completion of it.

He watched the man go through the rain and held

the envelope in his hands. He felt soiled by it. And he knew then that he would find the address of the woman, who in his head he now called Ani, and give it all to her. He knew very clearly that he didn't want it, and that he had very nearly died for it.

As he turned to leave the beach a

strange thing happened. He remembered some things very clearly. He remembered the whale that washed up on the shore when he was just a boy and how there had been a great gathering of people to help lift it back to the water, and how he had thought then that there was a great sense in people of the right to life. He remembered the first time, with Danny's father, the man sitting on the side of the boat and passing him the raw fish on the knife and his first nervous taste of it and his dislike of it at first, and he was sure he tasted it then, though he might have tasted no more than the salt rain driving thickly off the sea. And he thought of watching the hares fighting, and how he was sure he had felt that fight somehow in the ground as he watched them. This life fight, he thought. Just things trying to live. And he thought of Danny, and he thought of her, her lifting shirt in the breeze and the surprise of her freckles, and he remembered intently the sense of pride that was in his friend and that he would never do anything to damage. It was Cara's face, though, when the flash came.

He heard this thump. The thud of a body landing. Hold could feel coming from himself this sense of a completion, and it came with something that felt like a permanence of himself. He felt the great human sense he had when he released fish back into the water, of letting a life go free for the few moments before they swam down from the surface. Then he saw her face briefly with this great desperate clearness and thought 'That's it.' He heard the suck of wet sand as the man jumped down. 'You're free. You're free of me now.' He had this strange sense of relief, as if a responsibility was leaving him, but it was coloured with this great and massive sadness.

The big man seemed to hesitate clumsily in front of Hold as if he was caught for a moment in the solidity of the man before him; and then he shot him. He shot him through the envelope and into the face and after Hold hit the ground there were little bits of Jiffy bag and tiny specks of money hanging in the air for a while like feathers, like a big bird of prey had just hit something mid-flight.

The crash of the shot in the bay shifted

out, ventriloqual in the thinning fog and abstracted,

and by the time it reached people it was shapeless and indistinguishable from the noises of the port.

It didn't feel right not using the silencer and the big man had hesitated clumsily and braced himself for the noise and then shot and the crash of the shot sat in the bay of the beach.

There was an obliteration to it and some vague prettiness with the flakes of money falling down.

The man called Stringer came back down the beach and picked up the destroyed envelope furiously and took the phone from the dead man and he stuffed them into his coat with the drug packets.

He was nobody, Stringer was thinking. *He was just a flunky.*

Then he took the gun off the big man and they went back up towards the taxi.

The big man was beginning to worry about getting back on the boat already and the ring of the shot still sat in his ears. He was getting the chills already thinking of the trip and looked disturbed.

'What's up with you?' asked Stringer.

The two men got into the taxi and it started off and went on towards the port.

By the time the tide turned, as the water slid

finally across their footprints and the body on the beach, the Irishmen were gone.

Inside the window of the van, the beetle lifted itself to taste the air and stilled itself as it sensed the movement of the taxi going past.

It scuttled to the edge of the window against the seal and worked along looking for an exit. No way out. It sensed that. Once in it, there's no way out.

On the beach, from the wet body, the blood soaked into the sand.

*

The card seemed reluctant to catch

and curled almost coyly from the lighter then the flame gripped it and the cover blistered, the gold line of the eagle deforming in some grotesque spasm as the passport caught fire.

The pages inside sucked up the flame and the man dropped it onto the damp ground. It burned for a while against the harbour sand, the covers more resistant, coughing up spells of flame in the ground-level breeze, the ashes kicking away from the pile.

As its weight lessened the passport turned two somersaults and sat tent-like on the sand and the cover burnt anew, a violet flame budding along the document's spine. The eagle curled in one final arch as both covers yielded to the catastrophe and crumpled into fire, and there, on the sand, Grzegorz's face looked briefly back to the man, wrinkled in the heat into this extraordinary grief, and then ignited.

The man put his foot on the remaining pile and crushed the glowing ashes into the sand.

Epilogue

Stringer stood on the boat and looked down at the wet and damaged money and felt this spit of fury. He thought about the crash of the shot and whether the body had been found and steeled himself for the call.

I'll just tell him we did exactly as he said. He wouldn't know I'd taken them. The tide could have got them. I just have to be careful moving them on.

He could feel the drugs taped under his arms and they seemed to exaggerate his heartbeat. They seemed to call to him somehow, egg his little germ on.

'There's just the big man.'

He turned round and saw the big man prone on the bench and sick and drained and then he looked down at the destroyed money furiously again. They were just recently out of port and he could see the myriad lights that were on in the fog.

'I could put it through the wash,' he thought. 'I could put it in some tights and put it through the wash. I'm sure they'd change it then. They'd just think it was damaged in the wash. I could send it in in little lumps.'

He felt proud at the idea. 'I've got brains,' he thought. 'I'm going to get ahead now.'

He took the heavy litre bottle out of the ferry shop carrier bag and peeled off the gloves and put them into the bag with the phones and the torn Jiffy bag and then he took the round beach stones from his pocket and put them also in the bag, tied the top and threw it out into the water. It fell for some time and for a moment ballooned and struggled as it hit the water and then it was swallowed up and disappeared.

Stringer looked around him. The light was fading now and it was unpleasant with the rain and the light faded early in the unpleasant weather. There was no one else on deck, just the big man.

'Jesus, look at you,' he called over. The big man called Galen was cowed and shaking on the bench under the air vent, his big bulk looking strange and in some ways childlike to be so vulnerable, as if he had been weeping.

The packages seemed to throb with their own heartbeat against the chest of the small priest-like man.

'Come here,' he called. 'Get some proper air. You're getting all the fumes there.' Both men were wet from the unpleasant thin rain.

'It's my break right here,' thought Stringer. 'I've got some catch up.'

The packages seemed to have a wilful energy of their own now, as if some need to progress, and they seemed to call to Stringer. He could hear this voice.

The big man looked up. It was as if he was bereft of some great thing. He looked up at the small man standing by the railings.

Below the men, a raft of guillemot scattered off the water as the huge boat went by, inexplicable to them the fifty thousand tonnes of metal cruising through the saltened water. They circled for a while as the thing went past, skimming low over the waves as the thing proceeded, and then, one by one, they dropped back into the water, having seen some thing of wonder.

'Come on,' called Stringer. The big man had got up now and was coming awkwardly towards him and as he came the small man braced himself. The big man's face was wet with rain and he looked dampened down and somehow smalled. He remembered those eyes, the way the big man seemed to leave them in him that time in the café, but he braced himself. 'This will be enough for him,' he thought. His grip tightened on the neck of the bottle. 'There's just him now.'

ACKNOWLEDGEMENTS

Thanks to Jacob, for help with the key Polish phrases, which were *vrooj prosser checkham*, and *gzie yesters?* They mean, in turn, 'come back to me', and 'where are you?' But they mean it very strongly.

Also, thanks to Simon for the chat about the boat, and in a roundabout way to Mick Kelly, who gave me my first net.

As always, C.H. Thanks also to Caroline Oakley, more for the quiet egging on than anything, and to Euan, for the long game.

Also by Cynan Jones

The Long Dry

'Jones's sense of place is acute, and his passion for the landscape – for its colours, its creatures, its textures, its scents – is absolutely magnetic.' **Sarah Waters**

'A paean to the corruptibility of the flesh... characterised by moments of startling imagery and stirringly intense lyrical beauty... a wee, wonderful book.' **Niall Griffiths**

'Combines clarity of style with deep thoughtfulness and symbolic richness.' **Robert Nisbet**

'Like looking at an impressionist painting. I'm in awe. Jones has written a stunning book.' **Jo Verity**

'The best f**king book I've read this year!' **Andrew Davies**

'As in William Faulkner's most moving work, Jones seemingly surveys the whole of existence by describing the humblest details of life... this is a powerful and highly recommended debut.' *Library Journal US*

'Bold and punctuated with some scintillating imagery, this is a near perfect debut.' *Western Mail*

'A convincing glimpse of life in all it's beauty and sadness.'
Big Issue

'A serious, thoughtful and, at times, genuinely moving work.' *New Welsh Review*

PARTHIAN

www.parthianbooks.com